"Quin[...].
I met[...]

I sat up so fast that I startled my dog, who looked at me reproachfully. The only time Dash likes fast movement is when he is running.

"Yes, I remember you." How could I forget? His dark hair and perfectly muscled body shimmered in my memory.

"I couldn't get you out of my mind after we spoke the other day."

I'm unforgettable. Good. This is very good.

His voice reminds me of hot caramel—thick, rich and buttery. Very smooth. And very sophisticated.

"I think you may be perfect..."

My heart skipped a beat.

"...for my son's tutor."

Books by Judy Baer

Love Inspired

Be My Neat-Heart #347
Mirror, Mirror #399

Steeple Hill Single Title

The Whitney Chronicles
Million Dollar Dilemma
Norah's Ark

JUDY BAER

Angel Award-winning author and two-time RITA® Award finalist Judy Baer has written more than seventy books in the past twenty years, including the bestselling Cedar River Daydreams series, with over 1.25 million copies in print. Her next Steeple Hill single title will be *The Baby Chronicles,* to be published in September 2007. A native of North Dakota and graduate of Concordia College in Minnesota, Judy currently lives near Minneapolis. In addition to writing, she works as a personal life coach and writing coach. Judy speaks in schools, churches, libraries, women's groups and at writers' workshops across the country. She enjoys time with her husband, two daughters, three stepchildren and the growing number of spouses, pets and babies they bring home. Judy, who once raised buffalo, now raises horses. Readers are invited to visit her Web site at www.judykbaer.com.

Mirror, Mirror
Judy Baer

Steeple
Hill®

Published by Steeple Hill Books™

STEEPLE HILL BOOKS

Steeple Hill®

ISBN-13: 978-0-373-87435-4
ISBN-10:   0-373-87435-9

MIRROR, MIRROR

www.SteepleHill.com

Printed in U.S.A.

Charm can fool you, and beauty can trick you. But a woman who respects the Lord should be praised.

—*Proverbs* 31:30

For Brenda and Larry Halvorson, who care for my horses as if they were their own. Thanks.

(Also, in memory of Cocoa, Duchess, Keturra, Gremlin, Sasha, Amigo, Nixon, Kennedy, Bird, Fish, Ole the Lamb, Domino, Mischief and all the other animals I've loved before.)

Chapter One

My question is this, if your home is your castle and your body is your temple, which gets more maintenance?

For me, *diet* is a dirty word.

Not to my roommate Maggie Tamburo, however. She puts notes on our bathroom mirror like the one hanging there today.

Someday I'll weigh what my driver's license says I do.

I pulled the sticky note off the bathroom mirror, wadded it up and tossed it into the garbage. No time to think of my roommate's hang-ups now. It could take hours just to run through the highlights, and I have an appointment today that I can't miss. I'm a part-time tutor and I have a little guy named Nathan waiting for me whom I can't stand up.

After my session with Nathan Tracy, his mother, Linda, caught me in the hall outside his room. "Do you have time for coffee, Quinn? I'd like to talk to you."

She beckoned me to follow her to the kitchen, where streams of sunlight poured over a blue-and-white checked tablecloth on a bright yellow table. She poured coffee, set out a plate of lemon-frosted biscotti and doughnuts covered with chocolate sprinkles in front of me and sat down.

"Nathan adores you."

"The feeling is mutual. I think he's going to be president of the United States one day."

"He'll acknowledge you in his inaugural address, I'm sure."

Linda's forehead puckered in thought. "There is a man in our neighborhood who could use someone like you. Jack was widowed two years ago. He has a ten-year-old son with juvenile arthritis. He's been trying to be mother, father, breadwinner, cook and housekeeper in addition to homeschooling Ben when he's sick, just like his wife did."

Linda sipped her coffee and pushed the doughnuts my way. I took another. Maggie would have a fit, but I don't gain weight—she does. Since I end up on her diet at home, I have to forage sweets for myself when she's not around.

"If you want my theory, he keeps busy so he won't have to think about having lost his wife, Emily. They were a 'perfect' couple, so in tune with each other that they could finish each other's sentences. Emily always said that if she thought about ice cream the next thing she knew, Jack was bringing her a bowl from the kitchen."

Linda leaned forward and rested on her elbows. "I know you are busy, Quinn, and that you work at two jobs, but I'm wondering if you have time for one more student."

Busy is an understatement. I'm a model as well as a tutor.

I have the natural Nordic look popular in the upper Midwest—tall, blond and leggy. My grandmother describes me as she might a really good dessert— peaches-and-cream complexion, honey-colored hair and naturally rosy lips the color of fresh strawberries. It's nothing I can take credit for, of course. God and my genetics get that.

My roommate Maggie Tamburo is also a model. While I model part-time for the fun of it, she makes her living in the business. Maggie is dramatic looking in a dark, exotic way reminiscent of Sophia Loren. She's voluptuous, sultry and prone to gaining weight easily, a problematic trait for a model who spends a lot of time in front of the camera. She has large brown eyes and pronounced features which are, when arranged as they are on Maggie's face, breathtaking.

"Modeling seems like a glamorous profession, yet you prefer to tutor. Why?"

"Looks are fleeting, Linda. What I can do for these kids can affect them, their families, maybe even the world. Someday I'd like to earn enough money modeling so that I don't have to charge so much for my tutoring services to families who are already financially strapped."

"You'd love Ben Harmon. He is an unbelievable charmer," Linda continued. "His father, Jack, is determined that Ben have the best education he can under the circumstances."

I felt a familiar pull toward this child already.

"Ben is the cheeriest, funniest, most thoughtful little boy I've ever met," Linda continued. "A sunny disposition personified. His mother once told me that even when he was in pain, he tried to smile through his tears." She put her hand to her chest. "It makes *me* cry when I think about it. Jack Harmon is stubborn in some stereotypical jocklike ways," Linda admitted. She bent her elbow as if to show off her flimsy bicep. "'I can handle it myself,'" she mimicked. "That sort of thing. Maybe he won't even consider it. He's an independent guy."

"I like him already." Independent men don't bother me. I'm independent, too. I only answer to one guy, God.

At that moment I caught a glimpse of a jogger running by Linda's kitchen window.

"Look at this," she said, rising to her feet. "Speak and he appears. You're going to get the chance to meet Jack and take a look at him." Her eyes twinkled. "And there's a lot to look at. He's the best scenery in the neighborhood. Wait and see."

Linda opened the door before the doorbell rang. "Hey, Jack. You must have smelled food on my table. Come on in."

"I'm pretty nasty." There was pleasant amusement in his tone. "I don't think you want sweat on your chairs."

"A little sweat never scared me. Besides, there's someone here I want you to meet."

Linda returned to the kitchen with a trim, muscular man with dark hair that curled into damp ringlets at the nape of his neck. A forelock drooped agreeably over one eye. He was tan, fit and lean, with a blatantly athletic body, even features and a wide, playful smile.

I understood immediately what Linda meant about improving the scenery.

"Jack, I'd like you to meet Nathan's tutor. She's been working with him ever since the car accident that's kept him home from school. She's amazing, by the way. Brilliant as well as beautiful."

"If she's as good a teacher as she is lovely, then Nathan is one lucky boy."

I clapped my hands to my cheeks and felt them burning. "Please, you two. You're making me blush." I reached to shake his hand and I felt engulfed in his firm, steady grip.

"And Quinn, this is my neighbor, Jack Harmon. He has a little boy who is slightly younger than our Nathan. He got none of his father's bad traits and all of his good ones."

Jack laughed and dropped into the chair across from mine. "Does that mean the poor kid has no traits whatsoever?"

Linda set a bottle of water in front of him. He opened it and chugged the entire thing down. "Oh, there's a redeeming quality or two in you."

She turned to me. "You're a fabulous father for one thing. I told Quinn how you homeschool Ben when he's not able to be in the classroom because of his juvenile arthritis."

"Impressive," I said, and meant it. That raised Jack's stature in my eyes. I love hands-on parents.

"Ben's worth it." Jack's expression grew soft with affection. "There's nobody quite like Ben, is there, Linda?"

"There's nobody quite like either of the Harmon men."

"You're the best, Linda." He reached for a biscotti.

Linda handed him a mug of coffee to dip it in. He ate it in three bites. "By the way, here's the address of Ben's dentist. I think Nathan will like him." He threw a business card on the table. "Thanks for the sustenance. I've got lots to do today so I'd better run—literally."

He turned his attention to me and for a millisecond I felt as if I were the one and only most important person on the planet. "Nice to meet you, Quinn. Keep up the good work with Nathan."

And as quickly as he'd come, he was gone again.

"Whew. That's a whirlwind of a man."

"Gorgeous, isn't he?"

"What makes you think I noticed?"

Linda hee-hawed. "I know you recently broke up with your boyfriend, so I'm sure you're reading the menu again. And your eyesight is good. You just can't miss a guy like Jack."

"Jack Harmon." I leaned back in my chair. "That name sounds familiar to me."

"You've probably heard of him through the fundraisers he runs. He's a big supporter of childrens' sport camps." Linda frowned. "I don't know how he keeps it all together."

She was silent for a moment. "Or maybe I do know how. Jack has closed himself off to relationships with women. By choice, he has no social life. He's a man still aching over the loss of the love of his life. No woman will ever be able to compete with Emily. They adored each other. What's more, it's easy to remember the good and forget the bad when you lose a spouse. Emily is flawless in Jack's eyes and always will be. No living woman can compete. I think he keeps the schedule he does in order to prevent himself from falling into that kind of temptation." She sighed. "Sad but true."

I put a business card on the table. "If you ever feel he wants help schooling his son, give it to him. When— and if—he's ready, he'll call me."

I stood and gave Linda a hug. "By the way, next time you go to the store, you'd better stock up on dowels and foam balls. Your son is planning to build the solar system before I come back."

"Not life-size, I hope."

As I left the Tracys', I stared at the large brick and stone houses along the manicured streets and wondered which of these enormous houses belonged to Jack and harbored two lonely males.

After my last student, I stopped by the Images photography studio and was greeted at the door with a hug and shower of kisses—some human, some not. The studio's resident pet, a long, lean greyhound named Flash, at my encouragement, put his paws on my shoulders and washed my face with his tongue. That done, he glided back to the couch in front of a small television and resumed watching a black-and-white rerun of *The Andy Griffith Show.* Andy's whistling has a mesmerizing effect on him. A rescued former racing dog, Flash has forsaken speed for the good life of a couch potato.

I own Flash's friend Dash, another Mayberry fan and an equally lazy greyhound who hogs my bed and steals my heart. My childhood friend Pete Moore, owner of Images, read an article on former racing dogs in desperate need of homes and took me to "meet" a few at a function at a local pet store one Saturday afternoon.

I, who needed a dog like I needed cellulite, immediately fell in love. If there is a more elegant dog on the planet than a greyhound, I don't know what it might be. Handsome, lean, athletic, intelligent, polite, loving… how could I go wrong? Frankly, I've dated very few men with all those qualities in one package.

Pete, who never minds kissing my cheek after Flash is done, grinned at me. "I am so pleased you're here."

"If I'd known you'd be so glad to see me, I would have stopped by earlier." I gave him a return kiss. "Got any work for me? I'm in between agents and Pete's been helping me out until I get a new one."

"Something is in the pipe, but I can't tell you about it yet." Pete's dark eyes glittered. "Very exciting. Very big. *B-I-G*, big."

"And you never exaggerate." I headed for the refrigerator at the back of the studio to get a soda. Flash looked up briefly to see if I was getting something for him, but Andy started whistling again and I lost his attention.

"Of course not! Except when I'm excited."

"Like now? Can you give me a hint?"

"My lips are sealed." He made a zippering motion across his mouth.

"Pete, you haven't had sealed lips since the day you got your braces off." Darkly handsome and dressed in his usual uniform of black trousers and a white shirt, Pete exuded pent-up enthusiasm. I can always tell by the erratic way he taps his foot that he's bursting with news.

"Okay. One hint. *T-E-L-E-V-I-S-I-O-N*."

"You are a still-print photographer."

"I didn't say *I* was doing this. I do have connections in high places, however. It could be something big for you if you wanted to pursue it. They are looking for a beautiful woman to host…" His eyes widened. "Forget I said that."

"Gladly. I'm not Maggie, remember? I don't go berserk at the notion of another job opportunity or worry that it might be my last."

Pete sighed. "She was in here the other day asking me if her nose was too big."

"And you said?" I sat down on the chair behind the desk in Pete's office and started digging in his desk drawers. He usually has M&M's hidden somewhere.

"I said it was perfect, that it matched the rest of her."

"Then she said?"

"That my statement was tantamount to calling her fat. On her last job someone said she needed to lose a few pounds. Therefore, if her nose matches the rest of her, then it is definitely too big, like the rest of her. Instead of making her feel better, I think she ran off to Weight Watchers to see if her nose could join." He shook his head. "How a person so beautiful and so insecure came to exist, I'll never know.

"Modeling is a lousy career for Maggie. She's strung out by too many self-confidence issues." He eyeballed me appraisingly. "That's why you're perfect for it, you know."

"Because I don't care what others think about how I look? Or because I have a thin nose?"

"Because you radiate an aura of 'take it or leave it.' Those blue-green eyes of yours change like the weather—

icy, warm, unreadable and frosty again. That translates onto film as incredibly mysterious, an ice princess who harbors warmth and passion beneath her cool exterior."

"How poetic." I grinned at him. "Of course, you're making it all up."

Furrows grew between Pete's eyes. "I don't think so. You only care about modeling because it allows you to run your tutoring business. It's a means to an end for you. That's what comes through. Coolness and passion, bodily presence but emotional detachment. I can't explain it, but it works."

"It certainly doesn't define me, if that's what you mean."

He pushed a portfolio at me. "See for yourself." It was his collection of photos of me in all the ads I'd ever done. Actually, it was my personal portfolio, but I left it at the studio most of the time. I pushed it back to him unopened. I refuse to keep it at home like a little shrine to myself. It's my work. It's not me.

I thought of Maggie's bedroom. There were photos of her hung everywhere. Oddly, she displays those of herself she likes *least* rather than the ones she likes best. She says they are reminders of what *not* to do. I couldn't live in that negative swill, but Maggie insists it keeps her going. Maggie grew up in a negative environment where body issues were concerned. Her sisters put her—and each other—down rather than building everyone up. They leeched every bit of self-confidence from her.

The fickle public is never going to give her what she needs. She needs to know she's valuable no matter how she looks and only God can show her that.

"Can I be frank with you, Quinn?" Pete's dark eyes were somber.

"Aren't you always?"

"I'm usually full of drivel and you know it, but this time I'm serious. I'm really concerned about Maggie."

Pete, Maggie and I have been friends for a long time and I trust his instincts where Maggie is concerned.

"This insecurity thing is getting out of hand. She's convinced herself that if she had a different look she'd have more jobs."

This is a long-running conversation between Pete and me. "Maggie is never short of jobs for long. The problem with two models living together is that they seldom have work at the same time. I wish Maggie would quit keeping track of every time I've got a job and she doesn't. Maybe I should quit modeling altogether so that I'm not in competition with her."

"That would be a big help," Pete said sarcastically. Then he leaned back and studied me. "And there it is again, that 'take it or leave it' attitude that makes you so mysterious and desirable as a subject."

"Whatever. This isn't a conversation about me, Pete. It's about Maggie."

He leaned forward and put his hands on the desk. "Frankly, Quinn, I think that if we don't convince Maggie to start liking herself she might do something stupid."

"Something stupid? Like what?"

"I don't know. I can't even tell you why I say it other than I've known Maggie since before she could tie her own shoes and I don't like the direction she's going."

Me, either. But is there anything I can do to stop it?

Chapter Two

"Quinn, are you home?" I heard Maggie come through the back door and begin to rummage around in the kitchen.

Dash, in residence on the couch, opened one eye and shut it again. I have area rugs that move more than Dash.

It's remarkable that an athlete like a greyhound that is able to run up to forty-five miles an hour can be so mellow and laid-back. The only adjustment Dash had to make to my place was learning to climb the stairs. Dash had never seen stairs before and watched me go up and down several times before he tried it himself.

I live in a suburb of the Twin Cities in the home that my grandparents shared until they moved to senior housing. Now I mow the lawn, tend hydrangeas and peonies and shovel the sidewalk while they take computer and French-cooking classes in their new place.

"Hey!" Maggie greeted me, a banana halfway to her mouth. "Did I get any calls?"

"No. Sorry."

Her dark eyes narrowed. "But there were for you?" Maggie got my share of competitive spirit as well as her own.

"A couple," I said vaguely.

"Don't hold back because you think it will hurt my feelings that you got a job and I didn't. Spill it." Maggie is always happy at my good news, but it's a double-edged sword. Every job I get is one she didn't.

"I got a call from a local designer who is planning a new catalogue. Should be fun if I can fit it in."

"What do you mean 'fit it in'?" Maggie's brown eyes grew wide and her mobile face displayed a host of fleeting emotions—envy, regret, hopefulness and ultimately, good humor. "I'd give my teeth to do a catalogue!"

"If you give up your teeth you aren't likely to get into any magazine but the trade for American Dental Association."

Although everyone else thinks it is romantic and glamorous to model, I'd much rather build clay replicas of the Alamo with a fourth-grader recovering from surgery than prance under hot lights.

"At least I have the health-club print ads to look forward to." Maggie flung herself onto the couch, disturbing Dash, who, in a rare show of displeasure, opened both eyes to glare at her before dozing off again.

She wore jeans and a frothy multicolored top layered over a hot pink camisole.

"You've been in my closet again." I eyed the outfit I'd purchased last week at the Mall of America. "Didn't you promise that you'd let me wear my own new clothes first, before you got to them? Shades of high school, Maggie!"

"Oh, sorry."

"Sorry you did it or sorry you got caught?"

She grinned at me. "Both?"

I glowered at her and she added, "Don't worry. As soon as I get some money coming in from the fitness-club gig, I'll buy my own things and let you wear them."

"Right. You've been promising that since you were twelve years old."

Maggie was recently hired to be the face of a local fitness club. Soon she will be peering down on us from billboards in colorful leotards with an "I'm Fit, and You Can Be, Too" smile on her face. I hope that doesn't remind her that she thinks her nose is too big.

"I am so glad you got the job. It's perfect for you." It has also done wonders for her spirits.

She visibly brightened. "Just sitting on elliptical trainers and rowing machines will make me buff." She tapped a long, well-manicured finger on her temple. "By osmosis, or something. Didn't we learn that in school?"

"What can leak in can leak out," I warned.

She plucked a box of snack cakes off the coffee table anyway.

"Are you sure you want to do that? You know how hard you will be on yourself later." Pleasure for a moment, recriminations for a day, that's how Maggie works.

She hoisted a cellophane-wrapped cake in the air. "It's a celebration. I'm going to be the face of clubs all over the city. Everyone will think actually I work out."

Maggie rolled off the couch, scratched behind Dash's ear and headed toward her room with the Twinkies.

Modeling is about illusion. It's obvious to me when I'm facing the camera, with a wind machine blowing my hair away from my face or batting fake eyelashes that look like tarantulas when they are lying on my makeup table. I might inspire young women to run out and buy a new wand of mascara so they can look just like me, but I know that the sleek, glamorous dress I'm wearing is pinned, clipped and basted to my body at the back, the filmy fabric itches and the casual, wind-blown hair took an hour and a half to fabricate into a "natural" look.

One of the things I loved most about my ex-boyfriend was that he cared for me no matter how I looked. I tested him. The first time he came to my house to pick me up, I answered the door barefoot, with no makeup and my hair in Velcro-like rollers the size of cans of pork and beans, and the look on his face never wavered. But that wasn't enough to keep us together. Eventually we realized our values were just too different.

I made myself a cup of tea and recalled some of the earlier men in my life. In high school, guys fell into one of two categories. They either wanted a "trophy date" or were too intimidated to ask me out. The confident ones were usually so self-absorbed as to be no fun at all and the shy ones skittered away like baby mice when I ran into them in the hall. I either fascinated or terrified them in high school. Romance and I never had a chance.

Fortunately I always had Pete and Maggie, so I was never alone.

In college, things were better. My university had a great basketball team. For dating, that meant I had a much larger selection of really nice guys who were actually taller than me.

"What's up?" Maggie returned to the living room in pajamas covered with drowsy sheep.

"I met a good-looking guy today. Nice, too."

"Want to tell me about it?"

"There's nothing to tell. He's a widower with a son. And he's still in love with his wife."

"Ouch. There's no way to compete with that. How long has he been alone?"

"Two years. But it's okay. I'm not interested. I just thought he was a really nice man. His ten-year-old has juvenile arthritis."

"Aha. It's the little boy you're interested in."

"You know me, I'm a sucker for little kids."

"And I'm just a chump when it comes to men."

Too true. Maggie has been disappointed in love more than once. The most endearing thing about my friend— her open, vulnerable, loving personality—is also the thing that sometimes drives me crazy. Maggie's pulsing, unprotected heart is out there, lying on a platter for all to see and anyone to break. Pete and I are very protective of her. Sometimes we are the shell to Maggie's tender, defenseless and exposed "inner turtle." A weird metaphor, I know, but apt.

"Where are you going tomorrow? I know how you eat when I'm not around. I found burger wrappings in your car last time you were out."

"You search my car for telltale signs of junk food?"

She threw herself into a chair. "I like to sniff the wrappers, okay? I am so sick of being on a diet!"

I wisely refrained from mentioning the snack cake she'd just eaten. "Then quit."

"Right. Then I could do Volkswagen commercials. I could be the Volkswagen."

"Maggie, you have a great look. No one ever calls me 'exotic' or 'lusciously appealing.'"

"That is because 'luscious' is a synonym for 'chubby.' I should have stuck with landscape design or been a chef like my mother told me to be. Or a librarian. I would have made a great librarian."

"Chubby? You're a size—"

"Shh. Don't say it. Someone might hear."

"You are twisted, my dear. I've never met anyone so paranoid about their looks. Especially anyone as 'luscious' as you."

"Years of practice growing up in a critical family, Quinn. I don't expect anyone else to understand. Tolerate me, will you? Love me if you can, but at least tolerate me."

No one other than Pete and I could appreciate the full meaning of her cryptic comment, but we had lived it with her.

Maggie's parents are sweet, hardworking middle-class people who, in many ways, were like the ducks who were given a swan to rear in the story of the ugly duckling. Their two older daughters look much like their father and his masculine good looks do not translate well to the female gender. Maggie's twin sister, although an identical twin, is a pale copy of Maggie.

It is odd how two sisters can look so much alike and yet one is prettier, more vibrant and appealing. But that's how it is in Maggie's family—one incredible swan growing up in a family of perfectly lovely ducklings. Unfortunately, the ducklings weren't particularly happy to be ducklings. They, dying to be swans, always tried to sink Maggie as she swam. Even though she understands their issues on a rational level, it ate away at the foundation of her confidence.

More than once I've been tempted to climb onto my soapbox at a Tamburo family dinner and scream out 1 Peter 2:1. *Get rid of all malicious behavior and deceit. Don't just pretend to be good! Be done with hypocrisy and jealousy and backstabbing.*

"Leave a wasps' nest alone and you don't get stung," is Maggie's remark every time either Pete or I attempt to defend her. Wounded early, Maggie's only hope of true healing is in God, but she has to start believing Him.

She believes *in* Him, all right, but never relaxes fully into His care. She's like me on an airplane, never quite putting my full weight down. I know that airplanes exist, I'm just not sure how they fly and don't quite trust that they will stay in the air. Maggie believes in God, but she doesn't trust Him enough to give Him the wheel.

Our conversation dissipated into comfortable silence as she watched her favorite reality-television show. Bored by the inanity of it all, I studied her thoughtfully. She didn't seem any different to me—insecure, but no more so than usual. Yet Pete was worried. I cannot imagine what "stupid" thing he thinks Maggie might do.

I chalked it up to Pete's creative imagination and went to take a bath.

I met Pete for dinner the next evening at an All-You-Can-Eat-For-$7.99 place after a photo shoot. Pete and I usually go there once or twice a month. It drives Maggie crazy that our metabolisms can handle it, so we usually go on a day she's out on a date.

"How are Maggie and Randy doing?" Pete asked.

"I have no idea," I said cautiously. "As far as I'm concerned, the jury is still out about Randall Wilson."

"He's a good-looking guy in a sort of muscle-bound, sleeves-of-his-shirt-are-too-tight-and-appear-to-be-cutting-off-circulation-to-his-brain kind of way." Pete dumped enough ketchup on his meat loaf to make it look inedible.

"True, but I've never had a conversation with him that didn't consist of the words *yeah, cool* and *whatever.*" I stole a piece of chicken from Pete's plate. "But I don't know him very well, so it's really not my place to judge."

"I worry about it a little sometimes." Pete slathered jam on another biscuit.

"Maggie is head over heels in love with the guy but my instinct says Randy doesn't feel the same about her."

"I hope you are wrong."

Maggie has the idea that she's not complete without a man on her arm, that she's not "enough" on her own. Another blight bestowed on her by her sisters.

When I got home I fed Dash, who deigned to rise to

go to his dog dish but obviously considered it his stab at aerobic exercise. Then I finished gathering facts on Pluto—yes, it's the farthest orb formerly-known-as-a-planet from the sun; no, Pluto is not only a cartoon dog—and prepared a math lesson to go with it—If you weigh seventy pounds on Earth, how much do you weigh on Pluto? Four.

When I heard a key clicking into the lock on the front door, I glanced at the clock, startled to think that time had passed so quickly. Maggie must already be home from her date. Then I realized it was barely 10:00 p.m.

"I thought you didn't have dinner reservations until nine… Maggie?"

Her long black hair was a tangle and she scraped her fingers through it as she poised in the doorway, wild-eyed and frantic. Tears made tracks of mascara down her cheeks, which were aflame with emotion.

I pushed away from the table and moved toward her, but she bolted into her bedroom. "I want to die. I just want to die!" The door slammed behind her before I could reach it. The lock clicked into place and I heard her fling herself onto the bed and begin to weep.

"Maggie, don't lock yourself in your room. I'm here for you. What's happened?"

"Go away!"

Ignoring that, I pulled a chair to the door. "I'm going to sit here outside your room for a bit. When you're ready to talk, open it."

"Go away, Quinn!"

"It's okay. I'm very comfortable. Don't worry about me."

There is a method to my madness. Maggie, though impossibly hard on herself, feels guilty if she thinks she is putting anyone else out, especially me. "I'll be here when you are ready to—"

The door swung open and a disheveled Maggie glared at me ferociously. "You know I can't leave you sitting out here!"

"It's my house, too," I said more calmly than I felt. "And you're my friend. If I feel the need to sit out here, I will."

"But if you're out here and I'm in there…" A sheet of tears rained down her cheeks. "Oh, Quinn, what am I going to do?"

Chapter Three

I pushed past her into the room. Maggie's photo album was open on her bed. She had shredded all her photos of Randy and scattered them on the floor like confetti. As she paced back and forth, kicking at the scraps, she muttered words like *cad, lothario* and *lout.*

Maggie has an excellent vocabulary when she's upset.

Most Scandinavians I know keep a fairly good rein on their emotions. I am the first generation in my family to be what my mother calls "huggy." I tell my family I love them, kiss them when I greet them and ignore their stiff-necked "what if someone sees us?" ways.

Maggie, on the other hand, comes from a large Italian family that relishes drama. They enjoy waving their hands when they speak and emoting all over the place. Normally, Maggie and I balance each other out in this department, but tonight my calm reserve was no match for her fiery rant. Finally, I called Pete.

"You know that 'something stupid' you were worrying about?" I said when he picked up the phone.

"Maggie?"

"You'd better come over. I think she's on the brink of doing something that might fall into that category."

"What happened?"

"She left for dinner with Randy but came home early." I lowered my voice a little even though I knew that Maggie couldn't hear me with her face buried in a pillow. "They must have broken up. She's been crying and mutilating photos of them together. I can't get any sense out of her. She might do better if there were two of us here to calm her down."

"I never liked him much, anyway," Pete said sourly. "I'll be right over."

By the time he arrived, the shower was running in Maggie's bathroom.

"Cooling down," I murmured, and handed him a cup of black coffee. "She's alarming me. You know how she is. Dramatic. Volatile. Sensitive. And now this. She doesn't have a shred of self-confidence left. Her sisters and now Randy have seen to that."

"I suppose I shouldn't be surprised that she thought Randy's opinion was the be-all and end-all. She went to school to be a landscape designer. Why did she quit to become a model?"

"You know Maggie. She had something to prove. Her sisters told her it would be impossible for her. I wish she'd do something she enjoys rather than whip herself into a frenzy over a job that's only skin-deep."

We stared morosely into our coffee cups.

"Maggie is doing with the modeling what she's always done, Quinn." Pete sounded as weary as I felt over Maggie. "She is trying to make herself feel better by collecting compliments from others about her attractiveness. She doesn't feel it in herself so she needs bigger and bigger 'fixes' from others. What better way to get people to see you as beautiful than modeling fabulous clothes?" He slumped deeper into the chair I'd purchased in a flea market in Wisconsin. "No wonder she's devastated. There's no compliment in being dumped." She claims she doesn't even know the reason.

Pete is right. The emptiness in our friend can't be filled with approval, compliments or fame, only God. Unfortunately Maggie thinks she's so broken that even her Original Manufacturer can't help her.

We stared at each other miserably across the kitchen table and clung to our mugs of coffee as if we hoped they'd keep us afloat in a stormy sea.

Pete called the next morning to check on us.

"She's still sleeping," I told him. "She took the dog to bed with her. He's a great tranquilizer."

Dash is not only unfailingly sweet and genuinely comforting; he's also comatose eighteen hours a day and makes everyone around him want to fall asleep, too. A sleeping pill on four legs.

"Glad to hear it," Pet said, sounding relieved.

"I hope we convinced her that any man who breaks up with her because he found someone else deserves a Scummy, but it has to hurt." The Scummy is the award Maggie and I have always given out for our bad dates. It's like an Emmy or a Tony, but no one wants it on their mantel.

"How about you? Are you okay?"

"Just tired. I got up early to find some scripture that might help her." I poured myself a cup of coffee, sat down at the table and cradled the phone receiver between my shoulder and my ear.

"Pete, how did you and I find God when we were in college while Maggie missed the point of Him."

"She never thought she was 'good enough.' She's always waited to 'do better' before she approaches God."

"My mom insisted on cleaning our house before the cleaning lady came." I recall the puzzling behavior with amusement. "There's no way *I* would have cleaned my room if there were a chance someone else would do it for me. Refusing to allow God into our lives until we try to clean ourselves up first isn't much different."

"He can wipe away our dirtiness and sin and yet we don't allow Him to do it until we've tried and failed ourselves.

"It is reverse vanity, isn't it? Some people think they're too good for God, that they are okay without Him while others think they're too *bad* for God, that even He isn't big enough to clean up their messes—like Maggie."

"Pete, you're the best. Have I told you that lately?"

"About fifty times last night. I'm almost beginning to believe it. Listen, Quinn. Remember that *B-I-G* thing I was talking about? Why don't you come to the studio this afternoon, and we'll take a ride? I've got someone I'd like you to meet."

"What about…"

"I'd rather you came alone."

"I suppose I could. Maggie wants to go to her mother's for a couple days."

Pete's wary silence spoke louder than words.

"Don't worry, none of her sisters are there. Besides, you know how close Maggie is to her mother."

"I wish that woman hadn't been so blind to what was going on with her girls."

"Mrs. Tamburo doesn't have a mean bone in her body and she wouldn't believe any of her children did, either. Besides, I watched those girls work. They never teased Maggie when their parents were around. They were too crafty for that."

"Then get her on the road and come to meet me. Don't say anything about this to Maggie, okay?"

"What's so secretive that I can't tell my best friend?"

"Just don't, please?" He paused. "And I thought *I* was your best friend."

"One of two. Don't try to distract me."

"Okay, okay, but you still can't tell her."

That weighed heavily on me as I said goodbye to Maggie. Glad as I was she'd decided to get away for her own sanity, I was also relieved that she wouldn't be around when I met with Pete's mysterious friend. I'm not good at keeping secrets.

I probably could be better at it, but I've found that one of the best wrinkle-preventers is complete honesty. I never have to crease my forehead trying to remember what I've said. The truth is always easier than a lie. A great little tip for anyone in my business.

After numerous hugs and kisses and fervently acknowledging that Randy had made the biggest mistake of his life by dumping her, I watched a teary Maggie drive down the road to her parents' house.

Lord, go with her, soothe her and keep her safe!

Chapter Four

"I don't like this, Pete." My heart raced as Pete and I drove in his vintage Jag to the mysterious undisclosed location where Pete insisted my life would "change forever." Pete likes old cars. They need to be in tip-top shape and good-looking, but otherwise, the older the better. I've always thought it would be nice if men had the same attitude toward women—that they get better with age.

We passed one of the dozens of parks around the city and I saw a family of geese waddling down the sidewalk. A guy on a bicycle nearly crashed into a tree trying to avoid them. I've seen entire streets clog up while a mama and her babies made their way across the road.

Excitement fizzed around Pete like Alka-Seltzer in water, but the farther we drove the more concerned and uneasy I became. I like my life. Changing it forever isn't all that appealing to me—even if one of my best friends in the entire world might think it's a good thing.

"It's time to tell me what this is about, Pete. I'm not big on surprises. Since Maggie's not here, you can tell me what's going on."

"Relax, Quinn, you're in good hands. Would old Pete steer you wrong?"

"Aren't you the one that insisted a band could never be too loud to hurt your ears, that Enron would be around forever and that there was no possible way to improve on Oreos—just before they started making Double Stuf? And aren't you the one who insisted that we would wake up on the first day of January in 2001 and be back in the Stone Age, that Game Boy and iPod would never last and that high-definition television was just some geek's passing fancy?"

"Okay, so I'm not perfect one-hundred percent of the time."

"Pete, you're perfect zero percent of the time. Did you forget about original sin?"

He ignored that. It is well known that all of Pete's sin is very original. "I want you to promise me you'll keep an open mind about this. Don't say no until you hear them—and me—out."

"What do you take me for?" I asked waspishly as we passed the silver, yellow and blue cars of the Metro Transit light rail on the Hiawatha Line as it picked up passengers. "I've got a bad feeling about this already and I don't know where we are going or what we are doing. If you'd give me a hint…"

He sighed dramatically to indicate just how put upon he was and how patient he'd been. "The reason I'm not telling you where I'm taking you," he said with studied patience, as if he were talking to a recalcitrant child, "is because I'm afraid you might not go if I tell you. And if you don't go, you'll never know what an interesting opportunity this is."

"'Interesting opportunities' with you have, over the years, included that case of food poisoning we got from eating egg-salad sandwiches."

Pete looked injured. "I didn't think you could get food poisoning at a church bazaar—divine protection and all that."

I closed my eyes and a veritable parade of images marched before my eyes. The time I trusted Pete to convince me that skateboarding was easy and when I believed that he actually had taken dozens of slivers out of people's fingers. *Gullible* is my middle name.

"And you wonder why I'm suspicious. You've been dragging me into crazy schemes since we were kids. I should have learned by now and moved somewhere that wasn't so accessible to you."

"You love me and you know it. Besides, this is one time that you really can trust me."

How our friendship has made it this far without imploding was beyond me. God is our glue, no doubt about that.

"Here we are." We pulled up in front of the one of the Cities' finest hotels in the heart of downtown Minneapolis.

"Now that we're here," he eyed me cautiously, as if I might still jump out of his car and run, "and I've made sure you are going to meet my people, I can tell you the story."

"*Your* people? As in let's have your people contact my people and set up lunch? Very Hollywood."

"I'm glad you wore a suit." He eyed me appraisingly. "It makes you look…professional…reliable….sensible…in an eye-catching sort of way, of course."

"This had better be good." I crossed my arms over my chest and frowned at him, not liking the way this was going.

"Eddie Bessett and Frank Bernhardt are in town today."

"Good for them." If Pete had expected a dramatic response, he didn't get one. I'd never heard of either of them.

"Bessett and Bernhardt? B & B Productions? The largest, most successful producer of reality shows on cable today?"

"And I'm supposed to know them how?" I was beginning to feel a bit guilty for not being as excited as Pete.

"*The Dollar Show? Hide-and-Seek? 30 Days to a New You? Fairy Godmother?* Don't you ever watch television?"

I recalled a show on which people were given a dollar bill and told to turn it into as much money as they possibly could in a week's time. At the time I'd likened it to the parable of the talents in the Bible in which the good servants made their master's money grow while he was away and the lazy ones just sat around, awaiting their employer's return.

Hide-and-Seek, on the other hand, was basically an Easter-egg hunt for adults. The producers of the show hid cash and jewelry in unlikely places, and people had to find it.

"*Fairy Godmother?* Isn't that the stupid show where they land on someone's doorstep with a lady in a puffy dress and a tiara who says she's there to help them find a prince or princess and make their dreams come true?"

"That's the one. Isn't it great?" Pete beamed at me as if I'd won a spelling bee.

"Unless she lands on my doorstep and offers to do laundry, I'm not interested. Pete, those reality shows are mostly vapid, inane…"

He clamped his hand over my mouth. "Shh. You don't want anyone to hear you."

"Why? Are Misters B and B hiding in the backseat?"

"Practically. They're doing auditions. They're casting for a hostess for their new show *Chrysalis*. Their production crew's eyes are everywhere."

Chrysalis. At least that's a pretty name, much better than *The Dollar Show*. Of course, everyone loves to watch things that have to do with money.

I opened my purse and pulled out my cell phone. "I'd better check my messages."

Pete grabbed the phone from my hand and snapped it shut. "Pay attention, Quinn!"

"To what? This has nothing to do with me, Pete." He was testing my patience. "I know zilch…nada…about reality shows other than that they put people in ridiculous situations and tape them making fools of themselves for fifteen minutes of fame. If I want to see that, I can watch the news."

All this drama and intensity over…what?

"This is your big chance, your opportunity to get out

there and be seen. Quinn, you are a knockout. Drop-dead beautiful…"

"You make it sound like I have a rather violent appearance, Pete."

"You are a stunner!"

"See what I mean?"

"If you could get the gig as hostess for this new B & B production, it would guarantee that you would have as much modeling work as you wanted and television work, too. You'd be a minor celebrity."

As usual Pete let his overactive imagination and his love for me take him too far down a crazy path. "Very minor. What good would that do me even if I did want to audition…and I don't."

"Quinn, what do you want to do more than anything?"

Pete already knew my answer, of course. "To teach. To get to these kids who are isolated and falling behind because they can't be in school."

"What about your dream of starting a tutoring academy? What about helping dozens of kids a month instead of just a few?"

"Of course that's what I want! But I don't see how…" My voice trailed away. "Oh."

"The pay is good. You could start the academy *now*. They are starting with six shows. Quinn, it's perfect! You'd have time plus money for the other things you want to do." Pete sat back, crossed his arms across his chest and studied me now that he had my full attention. "And you have the look. You'd be perfect for this show. Perfect."

I squirmed a little. Too many compliments in one sitting and I'm ready to run. I can't help it that my features are well-proportioned, my teeth even and my hair willing to do whatever I ask of it. That's like bragging about having a belly button or an elbow. I can't take the credit for my looks any more than I think I might be responsible for a flexible, working knee or a good digestive system.

"You are making me very uncomfortable, Pete."

"This is not shallow praise, Quinn. This time, you are perfect. They are looking for a woman who is traditionally beautiful and who has not had any plastic surgery. A *natural* beauty."

"What on earth does that have to do with being a host on a television show? Everyone in fantasyland improves on nature."

Pete's pained expression finally got to me.

"Quit looking at me like a wounded puppy. You'd better just get on with it and tell me what this show is about. And why do they want someone who's not had plastic surgery?"

"The idea is that the hostess is a perfect specimen. She's who the contestants will emulate, the beautiful person they want to be."

"And why is the show named *Chrysalis?*"

"Because it is about taking someone from their ugly cocoon and turning them into a beautiful butterfly."

Perfect specimens—cocoons, butterflies—shades of entomology. "Maggie is the reality-TV buff. You should talk to her, not me."

An odd expression flitted over Pete's features. Then he opened the door of his car. "I think I'll let Eddie and Frank's staff explain this to you. I'm not doing a good job."

"It's 'Eddie and Frank,' is it?" I teased as he held

open my door. He relinquished the car to the valet and escorted me into the ultramodern foyer of the hotel. "When did you guys get so chummy?"

"Remember when I lived in California for two years after college? I used to date Eddie's sister before I moved back to the Cities from Los Angeles. His sister Kristy and I didn't last, but Eddie and I still call each other once a year just to check in. I hadn't heard from him for a while so I figured he'd gotten too big for me. Then he called to say they were coming here to search for talent. He thought that because I'm a photographer I could help him in his search for a beautiful woman."

He hurried me toward a bank of elevators. "And while they're talking to you, just think about starting your tutoring academy. If you don't take it, how long will you have to cut back your teaching hours while you earn a living wage?"

He knows how to get me where it hurts. I thought of Nathan in his big cast, of his mother Linda, of the children who couldn't get that kind of special attention. Flattery doesn't impress me but Pete goes for the jugular when he brings up my students. My footsteps were uncertain as we walked into the elevator.

B & B Productions had, it appeared, taken over an entire floor.

We walked off the elevator into a beehive of activity. There were lovely women—reality-show-host wannabes—sitting on chairs, couches and around the conference tables. People with clipboards and harried expressions dotted the area. Most were talking on cell phones and none were talking to each other. No one seemed to be enjoying the beautiful view of the downtown skyline or even the gigantic television screens on wide pillars. One individual did sit at a black grand piano plunking out a tune, but as soon as someone called his name, he jumped up and disappeared.

Eddie and Frank—Bessett & Bernhardt—B & B—were holding court behind closed doors, and an assistant would usher someone out and call in another hopeful every few minutes. Each woman was lovelier than the last. They went through the bevy quickly. At this pace, they would run out of hopefuls soon. Apparently Eddie and Frank were fussy.

Good. If they were that particular, I'd never meet their standards. They could reject me and I wouldn't have to have the no-I'm-not-going-to-do-this conversation with Pete. I owe him that much. Ever since I've known Pete, he has had my and Maggie's best interests at heart. If I could choose a brother for myself, it would be Pete. He's doing this because he thinks it is right for me. The least I can do is politely hear what the famous Eddie and Frank have to say.

In twenty minutes the room was empty of applicants. Eddie and Frank were efficient at weeding people out, I'd give them that. The thought cheered me considerably. We'd be home in time for me to walk Dash.

Then the young woman with the clipboard approached us. "Are you Quinn?"

"Yes, but how—"

Pete elbowed me in the ribs to quiet me.

Obediently I shut my mouth and stood up. Exactly what, I wondered, had Pete told them about me?

Chapter Five

Eddie and Frank were holed up behind the double doors that led to the master suite. The outer room was now empty of wannabes. Only worker bees wearing earbuds and muttering to invisible people in other parts of the country were left.

"Eddie's a great guy," Pete whispered as an assistant checked to see if the principles of B & B Productions were ready for us. "But keep your eye on Frank. FYI, he fancies himself a ladies' man and doesn't like to take no for an answer. He's a manipulator, according to Eddie, but he knows how to get things done in the business."

"Sounds like a real gem." Now I was doubly curious about who was on the other side of the door.

Eddie is a good-looking guy with a soft paunch around his middle and hair that looks as though it had been combed in a wind tunnel. He is pasty pale but, his blue eyes are sharp and astute. He strode across the room to embrace Pete in a gigantic bear hug. "Hello, you little weasel who didn't marry my sister, how are you?"

Pete reddened and I grinned. It's okay for him to have the tables turned on him once in a while.

"Good. Great…how's Kristy?"

"More beautiful than ever. You missed a good one there, buddy."

"I suppose she's married. Does she have a family?"

"Did I say she was married?" Eddie scowled at Pete. "For some unknown, unfathomable, ridiculous reason, you ruined her for other men. 'Pete did this… Pete did that….'" he mimicked. "You don't look like you have a romantic bone in your body. If I were a woman I wouldn't give you a second glance."

Pete appeared mightily relieved at that.

Then Frank stood up and rolled across the room toward us. Yes, rolled. Like an undertaker in B movie, the oily, smarmy kind that navigates across a floor smoothly and silently as he unctuously relishes the addition of one more body to his collection.

If Frank hadn't been a television producer, he would have made a great character in a haunted house. I don't often get a visceral response to people, but Frank immediately made my nerves jump. He looks the part of the emperor of cheap-shot reality television.

I don't mind the cute reality shows. Really, I don't. Thanks to Maggie, I watch the ones featuring aspiring singers and dancers. The rest? I'm not sure they're worth the fifteen minutes of fame the contestants get.

"So this is Quinn." Frank took my hand and kissed

it. Then he licked his lips like a snake flicking its tongue in and out.

It took everything in my power not to wipe the back of my hand on my skirt.

Pete made the proper introductions and we sat down in a cozy little ring around a coffee table littered with salted-nut-roll wrappers, paper coffee cups and dried-up sushi.

"So, Quinn," Eddie began, "Pete was telling me the truth. You are lovely. In fact, you remind me of my sister."

I eyeballed Pete and he shrugged.

"Thank you." I wished that Frank would quit staring at me as if I were sitting in an X-ray machine being scanned for defects.

"Did Pete tell you much about this show and what we're looking for?"

"Frankly, no. He seemed to think that I wouldn't come here today if I knew what you were up to."

Pete glared at me.

"It's a great premise, actually. You know, of course, that a chrysalis is the cocoon of a butterfly." Eddie's eyes lit with excitement. "That's what we're doing with the show—bringing people out of their cocoons, making them beautiful and showing the world what's been hidden until now."

"So it *is* another makeover reality-show."

"This is different. We're also going to track the contestants' emotions, the how and why of what they decided to do. We want to mine their emotions, make them real people, not just a nose-job or a tummy tuck. Not only will we make these people look great but we'll know *why* they choose the changes they do. It's about their thoughts, feelings and motivations. Who is it they want to emulate? Who are their heroes? It's about the whole person, not just the body. The beauty is just the frosting on the cake."

Frank took up the sales pitch. "It's the twist in the premise that's going to make the show catch on. The hostess of the show is going to be the contestants' role model. It will be a mentoring role, almost."

I still hadn't heard anything to convince me this show was much different from what was already on the television.

"These contestants will want to figure out what it is you have so they can have it, too. You know, charisma, charm, all that stuff. That's why we need the perfect hostess." Eddie leaned forward and impaled me with his baby blues. "You have it all, Quinn."

"And, of course, there's the grand finale." Frank is thin to the point of gaunt, with sunken eyes and a beak of a nose. He rubbed his hands together as he spoke, as if already mentally counting the cash that would roll in.

Pete leaned forward expectantly, already into this stop-and-chop way to beauty.

"The last show will be a beauty and personality competition. Which of the new butterflies is the most beautiful? Who exhibits the most personal growth? The winner will get a modeling contract and a cash prize."

"So you'll be exploiting people who don't like their looks and then pitting them against one another in a public competition?"

"Quinn!" Pete muttered.

Frank's face turned one of my favorite shades of scarlet. Pete was apoplectic but I ignored him.

"We'll make them proud of their looks," Eddie continued, unfazed. "What could be better?"

I looked at Pete's red face and refrained from voicing what I was thinking. *When pride comes, then comes disgrace but with the humble is wisdom.*

"I've heard about you ever since Pete started dating my sister," Eddie said smoothly, and sent a dimpled smile my way. He's sweet in a teddy-bearish way that's very disarming. "'My best friend Quinn…' 'Quinn says…' 'When Quinn and I were…' That's all Pete ever talked about. Sometimes I wondered why he just didn't marry *you.*"

Pete gurgled something unintelligible.

"Pete and I like each other too much to start dating," I said with a laugh. "There's nothing like romance to kill a good friendship."

"I like you, too, Quinn." Eddie studied me from beneath beetled brows. "I can see what Pete's talking about. You're lovely, but you are also solid and sensible. I could see it in your pictures but even more so now, in person."

"You've seen photos of me?" I turned. "Pete?"

"I just sent a couple, that's all."

I'll throttle him later. It would be much too messy to do it now.

"And now Pete has made up for his idiotic move not to marry my sister." Eddie turned to Pete, who was busy writhing uncomfortably on a low-slung couch. "He found our host for *Chrysalis.*"

"He did?" Then it dawned on me. Eddie was talking about me. "Oh, I couldn't. I'm not looking—"

"Quinn!" Pete's voice was strangled. "Don't say no without thinking about this! It's a terrific opportunity. What about the tutoring academy?"

"We've been auditioning all week and nothing has clicked," Eddie added enthusiastically, "but when you walked in here, I knew."

"Me, too," Frank echoed.

I tried not to fidget. The man is a character straight out of Edgar Allen Poe.

"There are lots of beautiful women, Quinn, but you've got something special. You can be a role model for these contestants. We want this show to be about an emotional—maybe even spiritual—change, as well as the physical one."

The very idea gives me the chills. People are shooting pretty low if it's me they want to emulate. Be like Jesus—that's one thing. But be like Quinn? The only thing I want people to see is Christ who lives in me.

Eddie wrote something on a piece of paper and slid it across the table to me. "Here's what we're willing to pay you."

I stared, dumbfounded, at the figure.

They'll pay me this to be a pretty face? Unbelievable.

Pete ushered me out of the suite quickly, volubly assuring Eddie and Frank that I'd consider the offer and get back to them. I didn't even have time to summarily turn them down.

Out in the car, he turned on me, his eyes flashing. "What were you trying to do, blow everything? I was afraid I wouldn't get you out of there without you turning them down flat!"

"I would have, but you hauled me out so quickly that I didn't get a chance. We don't need another television show that touts beauty and gives the message that people aren't okay unless they look like models. When are we going to realize that people need to do their cosmetic surgery on the inside first?"

"There's no way to get ratings with that." He flung himself across the wheel of the car. "You heard Eddie. This is also about emotional change. He was particularly interested in you when he found out you were a Christian. He said that would probably give you depth."

I massaged a sore point on my temple.

Fortunately Pete didn't pursue the conversation further, sensing that I'd reached my limit of patience. Although he wouldn't give up, he did know when to back off.

When I arrived at Linda's house to tutor Nathan, she met me at the door with a wide smile.

"You look pleased with yourself," I commented.

She started to hum that refrain from *Fiddler on the Roof,* "Matchmaker, matchmaker... He liked you, I could tell."

"If you are talking about Jack Harmon, and I know you are, I liked him, too. He's a very pleasant man. I wish him all the best. I congratulate you on having lovely neighbors. Now, if you'll excuse me, I have a job to do and your son is waiting for me."

"Jack didn't call you?" Linda's face crumpled in disappointment. "I thought he would. I thought he might like the idea of a tutor for Ben and then at least you two could get to know each other."

My head began to hurt again and Pete wasn't even around to blame.

"You said he's not over his wife."

"Even if you two weren't interested in each other, Ben could benefit from your help. When his mother was alive, they kept busy all day long. After their home-schooling stopped for the summer or when Ben was able to go to school, they just kept on learning. They visited parks, museums and the zoo. Ben and his mother went to every play at the children's theater and all the exhibits and the science and art museums. That child can already name all the Impressionist painters, identify their work and give biographies of their lives! Jack would take them to music in the park, concerts and rodeos. Emily taught him to play the piano and Jack helped Ben float on his back.

"But when Emily died of a brain tumor, it all stopped. Jack doesn't have enough hours in a day to be both mother and father. Even little Ben sees his dad burning the candle at both ends. He has actually told his father to ease up. Out of the mouths of babes, I'd say."

As Linda chattered on about Ben and his father, my mind drifted back to *Chrysalis* and to my wariness of anything that puts emphasis on outer attractiveness at the expense of inner loveliness.

Eddie wants a role model for the contestants to emulate, but what does that mean? Will people fake personality changes until the show is over or get down to the nitty-gritty and make lasting changes? And what about God? He is the only One who can create significant transformation in anyone's life. He did in mine.

Gradually I tuned back in to Linda, who was still babbling.

"Ben Harmon is so patient and cheerful despite his physical issues. I'm no expert on juvenile arthritis, but I know he has joint pain, swelling and a lot of stiffness, especially in the morning. Ben has fevers, fatigues easily and misses a lot of school. He goes through cycles when his condition worsens then, after while, he improves again. It's a roller coaster for both him and his father."

Linda poured more coffee and absently pushed a carton of cream my way. "Sometimes I weep for that little boy. He's such a trouper. He never complains, even when I know he is hurting."

"Did you know his mother well?"

"Emily? We were neighbors, of course, but because we had boys the same age, we ended up in a lot of the same places—the swimming pool, the playground, school functions.

"I remember when they first discovered Ben's illness. He'd come down with an unexplainable rash and a high fever. It was quite a shock to discover he had juvenile rheumatoid arthritis. They did a lot of blood tests and studied his bone marrow to rule out other conditions. Finally, they did a bone scan in an attempt to explain Ben's bone-and-joint pain."

"What can they do for him? I'm not terribly familiar with juvenile arthritis."

"Medication, physical therapy and exercise. They've

avoided injections and surgery so far. Emily was determined not to let the disease impair Ben socially or emotionally. She became as adept as Ben's physical therapist in helping him with range-of-motion exercises."

I tried to imagine how difficult life must be for this father and son. Ben Harmon was just the kind of child I wanted to help.

Chapter Six

As I got into my car, I recalled my conversation yesterday with B & B Productions. I could help a lot children like Ben if I had an entire team of tutors. I was already close to the maximum number of students I could take. I tried to swat the idea away like a pesky mosquito. Unfortunately, Pete's nonsense had drilled its way into my consciousness, like the words to an irritating song that just won't go away.

Just as I reached for the ignition, my cell phone rang.

"Quinn? It's me, Maggie."

"Hi, sweetie, how are you doing?"

"Going crazy. Why is it that the minute an adult woman walks into her mother's home she becomes a child again?"

Every time I visit my own mother, I go directly to her cookie jar. The first time I found *store-bought* cookies instead of homemade, I thought I would faint dead away. That, more than any other single event, made me realize that Mom had moved on—to the golf course, to the gym, to watercolor painting and to how-to-make-sushi classes.

"What's she got you doing?"

"Making my bed, washing my hands before dinner, telling her where I'm going to be every hour of the day…"

"That doesn't sound so bad. You make your bed and wash your hands, anyway."

"…cleaning my plate at dinner, raiding the cookie jar, drinking her sinfully good malts. I'm going to look like the Goodyear blimp before I get out of here."

I closed my eyes and suppressed a groan. She doesn't need ten pounds to add to the problems she's already dealing with.

"How's everything else?"

"My sisters haven't been around, if that's what you mean. It's the only bit of *good* luck I've had lately. I haven't asked what any of them are up to—flying off to somewhere on their brooms, no doubt."

Her voice grew soft. "Or do you mean has Randy called to beg me to come back? No." The breath she drew had tears in it. "Or are you asking if I've come to grips with the breakup?"

I knew better than that.

"What did I do wrong?" Maggie's voice broke. "What's wrong with me? He found someone prettier, taller and thinner than me, I just know it. Someone with a pert little nose and big blue eyes. A blonde. I'd bet you anything it's a blonde. I know he's not dating someone who looks like *me*."

"How do you know that?"

"What guy would? He just woke up and realized there was something better out there."

"There is nothing 'better' than you."

"You know what I mean," Maggie said obtusely, and wouldn't elaborate further.

"Snap out of it, Maggie. You aren't going to let Randy's bad taste influence you, are you?"

"Let's talk about something else." Maggie went into diversionary mode. "What have you been up to?"

I opened my mouth but closed it again. I was about to tell her about the *Chrysalis* interview but thought better of it. What she didn't need to hear today was about women so desperate to be different that they were willing to go on national television and put themselves in the hands of the sycophantic, smarmy Frank to make it happen.

News of a beauty contest was not going to cheer Maggie up, either. Telling her about it would be like opening the lion's den on Daniel if he hadn't been bathed in consistent prayer and praise. When King Darius's men tossed Daniel in with the lions no harm came to Daniel because he trusted God. When Maggie gets into one of these moods, all sense of prayer and trust seem to flee from her.

"When are you coming back? You had enough toiletries, makeup and hair supplies in your suitcase to stay a month."

"A month for you, maybe. I need a lot more support equipment than you do."

I bit my lip until I thought I might break the skin. Maggie doesn't even realize how she sounds, anymore.

"I'll be back soon. There's no use running away from this. Randy is gone. I only hope that my mother is right."

"About what?"

"That I'm 'better off without him.' She's said that a lot over the years and, in retrospect, she's usually been right. I think I'll come back to the apartment tomorrow evening," Maggie continued. "I've got to work out at the gym. Next week we start the shoot for the health club. I need to be in shape for that."

After we hung up, Maggie and her issues lingered in my mind.

Lord, help her, will You?

With Dash at my side I lay on the bed reading *Anna Karenina,* my current stab at the classics, when Linda called. Dash loves the classics. I think it's the smell of the leather bindings on my burgeoning collection. They are elegant both inside and out. Dash, from somewhere in his royal background when greyhounds were the chosen dogs of the queen must have gathered a little DNA that causes him to enjoy fine literature. After all, both Shakespeare and Chaucer made greyhounds famous. Dash knows style and sophistication when he sees it.

Greyhounds hold particular fascination for me because of what I call their "religious background." During the Middle Ages they nearly became extinct due to famine and disease, but they were saved by monks and priests who protected them and bred them for noblemen in their monasteries. They are also the only breed listed in scripture, which pleases me to no end.

Suspecting it might be Pete, I almost didn't answer the phone when it rang, Ever since our meeting with the movers and shakers behind B & B Entertainment and *Chrysalis,* he's been on my case nonstop to accept their offer.

Even though the money is tempting, it's not motivation enough for me to overlook the shallowness of the concept. Besides, although the mover behind the program—Eddie—is really quite likable, the shaker—Frank—makes me shudder. The man gives me the creeps. I've met a few weirdos over the years. Not every producer and photographer is a sweetheart like Pete. Frank is a composite of every bad experience I've ever had.

Funny, I don't usually jump to judgment. *Do not judge, so that you may not be judged and all that.* God and I will definitely have to have a talk about this.

My curiosity finally overrode my reluctance to talk to Pete and I answered the phone.

'Hi, this is Quinn."

"Quinn, my name is Jack Harmon. I met you at Linda's place."

I sat up so fast that I startled Dash, who looked at me reproachfully. The only time Dash likes fast movement is when *he* is running.

"Yes. I remember you." *How could I forget?* His dark hair and perfectly muscled body shimmered in my memory.

"I couldn't get you out of my mind after we spoke the other day."

I'm unforgettable. Good. This is very good.

His voice reminds me of hot caramel—thick, rich and buttery. Very smooth. And very sophisticated. I'm becoming like my grandmother, describing everything I come in contact with in terms of food. To her, not only is her mailman a "tall drink of water," but "sour as a pickle" and "a prune-faced" old grouch. Pete is "a dumpling" and my father, her "little pumpkin."

Or maybe I just need to eat lunch.

"I think you may be perfect…"

My heart skipped a beat.

"…for my son."

Oh, *that* Harmon man. Too young but intriguing, nonetheless.

"As you know, Ben has juvenile arthritis. When he is suffering muscle weakness and inflammation, he really isn't fit to go to school. When he's under stress or having pain, he tends to be less outgoing and doesn't participate as much."

"I'm sorry. It must be very difficult."

"We manage," Harmon said tersely, as if discussing this cut at him like a knife. "I'd like to visit with you in person, Ms. Hunter, and I'd like you to meet my son. If the two of you hit it off and if you have room for one more student, perhaps we can work something out."

"I'd be happy to." Not only was it a pleasant thought to see Handsome Jack, as I'd begun to think of him, but I was very interested in meeting his remarkable sounding son.

"What are you doing tomorrow afternoon?"

Avoiding Pete, mostly. Fortunately that shouldn't be too hard since he told me he was planning on going on a date with a woman he had recently met.

"I'm free after two o'clock."

"I'd like you to come to my home. I'll give you my address."

"It's a date," I said agreeably, then wished I could take

back my poor choice of words. I was talking to a grieving widower with an ill child and his lifetime of memories.

Unfortunately—for me, at least—the last thing this could be called is a date.

Chapter Seven

For as he thinks within himself, so he is. Proverbs 23:7.

I closed my Bible and stared out the window where a rash of finches, sparrows, grosbeaks and the occasional pileated woodpecker were scuba diving in the birdbaths and grazing at the six feeders I've put up for them around my yard. I keep a pair of binoculars on a nearby table and whenever I forget, even for a moment, just how wonderful God is, I pick up the binoculars and stare at the birds.

They are fragile, bold, determined, perfectly crafted little miracles. I particularly like to watch the goldfinches. Finches don't start mating until most other birds are done, waiting, instead, for the thistle with which they build their nests to mature. Yet when winter comes they are no farther behind than the birds that nested much earlier.

Our Divine Creator crafted us with equal attention to detail. We too can trust ourselves and our rhythms.

Sadly Maggie hasn't come to that yet. Her own beauty, intelligence and charm haven't helped her one bit because she doesn't think she is any of those things.

Dash, who can read my emotions faster than I can comprehend them myself, removed himself from his doggy bed and came to stand beside me. He leaned against my leg as if his nearness would drive away the sadness I was feeling over Maggie.

With my palm, I redirected Dash's nose back to his bed. "Dash, go lie down, honey. I'm okay."

Nothing doing. Dash planted his feet and leaned more heavily on me, sticking to my leg like a sixty-pound piece of Velcro.

"Let's go to Uncle Pete's, Dashy. He'll cheer me up and you can play with Flash. You can stay there while I go to my appointment with Jack Harmon."

He detached himself and ran to get his leash. *Go* is one of his favorite words.

First, I had to dig through Dash's enormous plastic bin of dog food for a set of spare keys I'd had made for Pete.

If a burglar came to rob me blind, Dash would not bark. Instead, he would accommodatingly show the thief where my cash, jewelry and car keys were stored. The only thing in the house that I know he would protect is his bin of dog food in the laundry room. Dash is emotionally attached to that bin and what it holds. He would make sure that, even though thieves moved everything I own into a semi and carted it away, the dog food would be left safely behind. Dash is a lover not a fighter, nor is he a self-respecting watchdog.

I'm no dummy. Anything I want to be safe, like spare keys, I put in a plastic sandwich bag, zip it shut and toss into the bin.

At Pete's studio, Flash was at the door waiting for us. He adores me because I smell like his buddy Dash. And because I carry doggy treats in my purse.

"Just in time," Pete greeted me. "I picked up bagels. You want yours with cream cheese, butter or dry?"

He pointed Flash toward the kennel, but the dogs had already heard the word *bagel* and headed straight for the kitchen. Not only do Flash and Dash know *sit, heel* and *stay,* they also are acquainted with *sandwich, ice cream* and *burger.* I suspect that there is really no end to their vocabularies but unless it is relevant to their stomachs or their comfort, they just don't let us pathetic humans know what they're thinking. Both dogs love to watch *CNN* and that terrifies me a little. What do they know that I don't?

"Cream cheese, of course, and strawberry jam—for the first half. Peanut butter and honey for the other half. Have you got French roast or Columbian coffee?"

"That's why guys like you so much, Quinn. You are robust, just like your coffee. I have cream, too."

We went to Pete's minuscule kitchenette at the back of the studio. He popped the bagels in the toaster and poured me a cup of coffee so thick and black that it resembled watered-down tar. I dumped cream in to the cup, stirred and tasted. Perfect.

"How was your date last weekend?" I like to start

conversations with the juicy stuff. "You didn't say how it went."

"Nice lady. No sparks."

"Will you see her again?"

"The question is, will she see *me?* If she has good taste, she probably won't. I was a pretty boring date."

"You're never dreary around me. In fact, I was going to talk to you about becoming a little duller. I don't want you coming up with any more of this stuff like your *Chrysalis* idea."

"It's different with you. I feel safe."

"You mean you were in danger?"

"When I date, I always feel as if I'm being looked over as husband material." Pete sighed. "One of these days I'm going to get my foot caught in a snare and it will be the last you see of me. Whoosh. I'll be sucked up into domesticity—mowing a lawn somewhere in the suburbs, coaching soccer and selling hot dogs at a booth in a parking lot to make money to buy helmets for an eight-year-old's baseball team. I know you'll never do that to me. Therefore, I feel safe."

"I had no idea men had so many troubles."

"It's a changing world, Quinn."

"Maybe you're too fussy," I suggested tactfully. "Maybe your expectations are too high. You do spend a lot of time with fashion models."

"Having a stream of beautiful women coming through the studio has taught me one thing, Quinn. Looks alone aren't enough." Pete looked genuinely sad. "It's that old Pharisees and whitewashed tombs thing. Pretty outside, but jaded or spoiled inside is not for me."

Woe to you, scribes and Pharisees, hypocrites! For you are like whitewashed tombs, which on the outside look beautiful but inside they are full of the bones of the dead and of all kinds of filth.

I got his point.

He glanced at a life-sized black-and-white he'd done of a woman in a designer evening gown. Her head was thrown back, her eyes heavy lidded and her lips wet and full.

He gestured toward the photo. "Between shoots all she did was argue with her boyfriend on her cell phone, scream invectives at him and threaten him with what she'd do to him when she got home. If I'd been that guy, I would have purchased a one-way ticket to Siberia before I'd take any more of that.

"My mother wouldn't have spoken to my father like that for anything in the world. She was pretty enough, but what was more important was that her heart was pure gold. She was crazy about Dad and he loved everything about her. *That's* what I'm looking for now."

I recalled the many hours I spent in Pete's home, playing Monopoly or putting puzzles together. His mother was always singing, always smiling. It's no wonder she raised such a son.

I gave him a hug. "I adore you, Pete. Beneath your sophisticated exterior you are a sentimental sap. I like that in a man, tenderheartedness, loyalty, respect for home and family."

"That reminds me. Have you heard from our other faux-sibling Maggie?"

I gave him the recap of our conversation. "She needs to get back here to her friends. Hopefully tomorrow."

"The Three Musketeers, together again."

I glanced at my watch. "I have to go soon. I'm meeting with a potential new client and his son. The man is a widower and his little boy has juvenile arthritis."

Pete whistled. "Tough. I hope he's smart enough to hire you, Quinn. You are a miracle worker with kids."

I stood up and kissed Pete on the cheek. "Thanks for the food and conversation. I'll pick up my dog later."

"Thank *you*. Everyone else who comes here won't even drink water because it makes their stomachs bulge for the camera. Someone who doesn't care about the calories in cream cheese is a refreshing change."

The Harmon house is larger and more impressive than I'd expected it to be, an imposing brick Tudor-style with a four-car garage and two basketball hoops over the driveway. Odd, considering Ben Harmon would have a hard time playing ball. I drove the car into the circular driveway in front of the house and parked near the front door.

The yard is a plush carpet and the shrubs and flowers have been meticulously tended, all of which I found very pleasing. I've been known to pick weeds out of strangers' flower beds, pinch back dead flowers and use a watering can or two. I had none of these urges as I looked at Jack Harmon's pristine yard.

Eager to work with a man who liked order, I stood expectantly in the doorway waiting for him to answer the bell. Needless to say, I was taken off guard when he answered the door looking as if he'd been in an explosion in Betty Crocker's kitchen.

Chapter Eight

He was covered with flour from head to toe. The abominable snowman of the suburbs. Frosty the Flour man.

"Is it two o'clock already?" Flour man glanced at his watch, but it was also enveloped in a coating of paste.

If I hadn't met him before, it could have been difficult to tell Jack's age with his hair flour-dusted to a dull gray. His eyes, peering out from the ghostly face were warm and brown, his cheekbones high, his features chiseled and his face strong despite the layer of Gold Medal.

"We lost track of time," he said by way of apology. "I thought we could whip a volcano together in no time. After all, we did a clay Brachiosaur in two hours and a replica of the White House in a weekend. But Ben insisted that he wanted his volcano to be *papier mâché*. Then he dropped the five-pound bag and it exploded like a…"

He took a breath and looked up. "And you don't care in the least how I came to look like Frosty the Snowman."

As he spoke flour shifted from his clothing onto the floor.

"On the contrary. I find it fascinating. I've made more than one or two science projects myself over the years. Once I did a study of eyeballs and went to a butcher shop to get…er, samples. Nasty. Very nasty."

"Whatever you do, don't tell Ben," his father said grimly. "Even I have some limits."

"I promise. Where is this budding Einstein of yours?"

Jack looked apologetic. "I'm sorry. You didn't come to hear this, you came to meet Ben. So far I'm not measuring up very well, am I?"

I didn't say it, but I thought he was holding up beautifully. Not only was he pleasant, funny, well built and handsome under the gunk he wore, he was working with his child on a project they could share. That's what counts with me.

"Come into the kitchen, er, the scene of the crime. Sorry for how it—and we—look."

He led me into a huge country kitchen with a granite-topped counter, a fireplace, a large old-fashioned table with a pedestal bottom and comfy looking upholstered chairs. The adjoining family room was an attractive mix of soft couches and chairs, a large-screen television, books, boxes of games and colored drawings all signed by Ben. Perfect.

A small boy sat on a stool at the kitchen counter. He was covered with even more flour than his father— closer to the bag when it exploded, no doubt—but I could make out tawny, gold-brown hair moussed into short spikes, a high, intelligent forehead and curious blue eyes. He was small for ten.

I eyed him surreptitiously, looking for signs of illness. Other than the slightly enlarged and reddened knuckles in his hands and some stiffness in his movements, he was a normal boy, curious about the stranger who had come to his house.

He smiled and his megawatt expression lit the room. "Hi, I'm Ben. Are you going to be my teacher?"

That took me by surprise. "Today, I thought we'd get to know each other."

"To see if we're a good fit?" Ben inquired like a thirty year old in a child's body. "That's what my dad says." The boy studied me intently, his blue eyes disconcertingly piercing. "But I can tell that I like you already and you're pretty, too. We need some new scenery around here."

Ben's father shrugged helplessly again and smiled at me.

"Since I like you, could you start being my teacher today? Dad's okay, but we could really use some help with this volcano."

I looked at the large square of plywood and the cone of metal screening stapled into it. They'd placed a cup in the hole that would be the crater, shredded newspaper and mixed flour and water for the *papier mâché*. There had been one pathetic layer of the concoction on the cone when the flour exploded.

"Looks like you two are doing fine. You'll need more layers of *papier mâché* on that cone before it looks like a volcano. Then it's just a matter of painting it to look like a mountain and making it erupt."

"That's the problem," Ben said, sounding as tested and tried as Job's patience. "If we keep doing it Dad's way, it will never look like a mountain. He just slops stuff on and says it's good enough. I think we should make it look like this." He pointed a grubby finger at a snapshot of Mount St. Helens pre-1980.

"It doesn't have to look like Mount St. Helens, Ben," Jack said. "The project is supposed to be a working volcano, not an authentic imitation of a real one." There was a comical expression on his face, half pleading, half proud, as if he didn't know whether he should throw up his hands over this determined child or stick his thumbs in his lapels and boast of the child's persistence.

I rolled up the sleeves on my pale pink shirt. "Your dad can start cleaning up the mess and I'll help you put on that second layer. If you have a small fan or a hair dryer, we can speed up the drying process. We can make this into Mount St. Helens without too much trouble."

"Awright!" Ben cheered.

"A take-charge woman, we like that," Jack said. "What do you want me to do?"

I looked around at the floury surfaces. "Vacuum, maybe? And how are you with a dust cloth?"

"I worked for a janitorial service in undergrad. I'm pretty good, if I do say so myself."

A man who knows how to clean a house? *Do you have a single flaw, Jack Harmon?*

"I'm glad you're here," Ben said, over the grinding sound of the vacuum as we put another layer of news-paper, flour and water on Mount Harmon which eventually, if all went well, would resemble the other famous mountain. "You're fun."

"Thank you. You're a lot of fun yourself."

"My dad is, too. when he's not working or worrying." Ben carefully smoothed the side of the mountain with the palm of his hand.

I glanced at him curiously. What exactly went on between those two cute ears of his, I wondered. This was an exceptional child—intelligent, mature for his age and sensible. His father deserves a lot of credit. Not everyone could use the hardships Ben's suffered to make him into such a wise old soul in a young, hurting body.

Jack finished vacuuming and returned to the kitchen. "Popcorn, anyone?" He looked at the emerging volcano. "Good job, you two! I wasn't sure it was going to happen for a while, but there it is." He smiled at me and I felt myself about to melt into a big puddle. "Thanks to you, Ms. Hunter."

"Quinn," I managed to say even though my senses were reeling. An attractive domestic male who is good at parenting and can wield a vacuum cleaner like a Merry Maid—I must be dreaming, I decided. And his cologne smells good, too. Things just can't get any better than this.

I glanced at the kitchen clock and gave a little gasp. Nearly two hours had passed.

"I had no idea it was so late. I didn't mean to move in and make myself at home."

At the front door Jack, his expression intent, reached out and touched my arm. "When can you start teaching Ben? Soon?"

"We didn't really have a formal interview. There might be questions you want answered before—"

"As far as I'm concerned, the past two hours were your formal interview. I'm perfectly comfortable hiring you to work with Ben."

Ben, in the background, gave a thumbs-up.

Jack's brown eyes sparkled with good humor and he reached to shake my hand. His fingers were warm as they cupped my hand. "Any woman who can move mountains, volcanic or otherwise, is worth hiring. Welcome aboard, Ms. Hunter."

I stopped at Pete's studio to pick up Dash. I knew Pete would be waiting to hear what had happened.

He'd just finished a photo shoot for a local jeweler. The model, a woman I'd worked with before, was wearing a bronze satin blouse with a plunging neckline that showed the necklaces to their best advantage. And, because all the photos were from the waist up, she also wore a pair of ragged blue jeans.

She took off the jewelry and handed it to Pete. "That's over."

She fell into step with me as I headed toward the back of the studio. "I hope I get more work like this," she murmured, as much to herself as to me. "It will give me time to get these thighs of mine back in shape. If I don't, no one will want to hire me to wear their clothes." Then she lifted a hand in salute. "See ya."

I couldn't help watching her as she walked away from me. I've seen ladies with upper arms bigger than this woman's thighs.

Pete put his hand on my back and I jumped. "Is she *still* complaining about her thighs?"

"Of course."

"It's going to happen until we quit sending the message that thin is good and anything else is bad," Pete observed gloomily.

"I find that very depressing. I'm waiting for Rubenesque models to come back into style. Ample features, plump cheeks and tummies—full, voluptuous women. Don't you think it's time? A full figure used to indicate wealth because that meant women were well fed."

"And then, as now, wealth was attractive. I wonder where the message got turned around so that thin and rich go together. Ironic isn't it?"

"It certainly is. It makes me hungry thinking about it. Do you have anything to eat?"

Finally Pete laughed. "No, but I know a great little Mexican place around the corner. Fresh tortillas, refried beans…"

"Sopipillas? Powdered sugar and honey?"

"If you pronounce it, you can have it."

Manuel's is a little hole-in-the-wall mom-and-pop operation decorated with garishly colored tile, stuffed birds and palm trees. The food is authentic and spicy, just the way we like it.

Over chips and salsa Pete began his third degree. "How's the new tutoring prospect? Do you think you'll get hired?"

"I already am."

"Just like that?"

"I hit it off with the little Harmon boy. It would be

impossible not to love him. He's fascinated by any- and everything and totally uncomplaining. I didn't expect that, knowing his condition. It certainly hasn't taken a toll on his sunny disposition."

"You've told me about the boy." Pete waved a waitress over to ask her to refill our basket of nachos. "Now tell me about the father."

"Pleasant. Easy to talk to," I said vaguely. "He mentioned being a stockbroker and he works out a lot. Linda said he coaches kids' sports."

"Good-looking, then?" Pete asked slyly.

"He's a client, Pete, not a candidate from a dating service."

"So he *is* a good-looking guy."

"What makes you say that?"

"Quinn, you are an open book. The corners of your mouth lifted a little, like a Mona Lisa smile."

So much for keeping secrets from a man who can read my facial expressions.

"How is Maggie?"

"Once the photo shoot for the health-club gig starts, she'll be fine. She's really counting on that."

Pete stirred his refried beans into a disgusting little pile that resembled Ben's volcano. "I saw Randy last night. He was out with a date."

My stomach tightened. "That didn't take long." I thought about Maggie's conviction that the woman Randy left her for would be young and blond. "Was she pretty?"

"Not really, not nearly as pretty as Maggie. Just an average looking woman. About five-feet-six-inches tall. She had light brown hair and a pleasant smile. Randy seemed dazzled. I would have said hello to him, but he only had eyes for her."

"Hmm." I dangled my fork over my plate and frowned. "What do you think made her so special that Randy would drop Maggie for her?"

Pete flushed and looked embarrassed. "I know why I would like her. I can't speak for Randy."

"Now I'm curious."

He sat back and chewed on his upper lip for a moment, choosing his words carefully. "She's not uptight."

That wasn't what I'd expected him to say.

"You know how Maggie is. 'Is my hair all right?' 'Do I have lipstick on my teeth?' 'Do these pants make me look fat?' And when you tell her she looks fine, she takes it as an insult.

"'Fine?' she says. 'Only fine? I worked for hours to look this way and it's just *fine?*'"

Too true. I'd heard it dozens of times myself.

"Randy's date appeared very warm and natural. If she had a compact mirror in her purse, she didn't bring it out." Now Pete really blushed. "Some guys appreciate that, you know."

Because Maggie makes her living being beautiful, it's easy to fall into that trap. A job-related issue, so to speak, one that has caught Maggie in its tenterhooks. She thinks nothing of checking her lipstick or fluffing her hair all evening long.

"When we go camping in the Boundary Waters in northern Minnesota, you know how she changes. Makeup free. Grubby. Natural. That Maggie is easy to be around."

"And the minute we see the first signs of civilization, she gets out her makeup kit and begins to stew about how she looks. What are we going to do about her, Pete?"

"I don't know anymore. I wish I did. She acknowledges that God is responsible for her features and attractiveness, but she doesn't trust that anyone—including Him—could care for her just the way she is."

"Maggie ignores her inner beauty for her outer one. Which reminds me, what are we going to tell Maggie about *Chrysalis?*"

"What is there to tell? I'm not getting involved. There's no reason to worry about it."

"Are you absolutely sure? This could be a huge break for your career."

"I don't want to build a television career on the backs of vulnerable people who don't like their looks."

"You make them sound like cave dwellers seeing light for the first time. The contestants audition and there's a tight selection process. You aren't protecting them from themselves by not doing the show. If you don't do it, someone else will."

"Why are you pushing this?" I felt suddenly snappish. "Is it because of Eddie and your former friendship with his sister?"

"It has nothing to do with her." Pete reddened. "I like Eddie. He's made good in a difficult business. He's an honorable man in a tough industry, despite what it may seem like to you. National attention will bring you bigger, higher-paying jobs. If this show works, there will be more income for you. That would free you to do what you really love—to build your own business placing tutors with students."

"Stop it!"

"Quinn, when you talked about that little Harmon boy earlier, your eyes lit up like stars."

I wish he'd be quiet. He's a little too persuasive when he brings up the children.

"I think it would be a perfect jumping-off point for your career." He leaned back in his chair and crossed his arms. The sombrero on the wall behind him framed his face and made him look like a bandito. "You know perfectly well that you would be an ideal hostess for the show."

I rubbed my temples. "Drop it, Pete. I can't think of a single circumstance under which I'd agree to do that show."

He shrugged helplessly and reached for the bill. Though disgusted with me, he obviously wasn't mad enough to refuse to pick up the check.

He loves me. He really loves me.

Chapter Nine

Dash loves it when I'm home and drilling through the television channels looking for something to watch. He—all sixty pounds of him—crawls onto my lap as if he's a cat. Although he may be big in size, Dash and many of his counterparts are lapdogs at heart. He curled his rump onto my thighs, propped a shoulder against my chest, laid his head against my cheek and exhaled noisily, a blissful, home-at-last sigh that encourages me to never let his delicate little paws ever touch anything as crass as hardwood floors again. If he could, he'd ride around strapped to my stomach all day in a giant baby carrier.

"So what is it? The Home and Garden Television or Discovery Channel? There's a special on rhinoceroses right now."

Dash whimpered a little and put his paw over his eyes.

"Home and Garden it is, then." He doesn't like anything with tough, leathery skin or horns. Offends his sensibilities, I guess.

We watched people landscaping, reorganizing their closets, discovering masterpieces in their attics and shopping for new homes. Dash fell asleep between installing a water fountain and cleaning out a garage. By the time I moved him, my legs had become heavy and numb as tree trunks.

"We've got to do something other than overdose on television, Dash. What do you suggest?

He scrambled off the couch and came back carrying his leash in his mouth.

Where Dash leads, I follow.

We managed to coordinate ourselves into a synchronized lope that gobbled up city blocks. Because our rhythmic walk is soothing and Dash, oddball dog that his is, rarely stops to sniff shrubs, signposts or small children, we covered the miles quickly.

My thoughts often sail along at the same rapid speed as my feet and today I couldn't keep from thinking about the television show *Chrysalis* and its allure.

Pride goes before destruction, and a haughty spirit before a fall.

It doesn't help that Eddie keeps sending me material about the show, dangling the proverbial carrot in front of the gullible donkey.

Weekly, before the audience's eyes we will release a new contestant from her ugly cocoon to reveal the beautiful butterfly that exists inside. On the final week, these stunning butterflies will compete with each other and the audience will vote on the most beautiful....

That's a recipe for bruised self-esteem.

Led by the leggy Dash, we found our way to Linda's

street, which is several winding trails away from mine. As long as we were in the neighborhood, I decided to see how Nathan was doing with his construction of the galaxy. Better yet, I could introduce the little boy to Dash. I'd spoken of my dog so often that Nathan had pleaded to see this doggy wonder of mine.

Linda was in the backyard watering flowers and Nathan was with her, decked out on a lawn chaise longue and listening to his iPod. Linda dropped the hose she'd been using and came toward us.

"Now, this is a surprise! Aren't you a little far from home?"

"I just kept following the dog and he covers a lot of territory. Since I was passing by, I thought I'd drop in."

"Can I see the dog?" Nathan laid his iPod on the grass.

Nathan reached out and Dash put his chin in Nate's hand and looked with big liquid eyes at the little boy. I could practically feel sparks as Dupid's arrows—my idea of a doggy Cupid—sailed between them.

"He's cool!"

"Troublemaker," Linda muttered under her breath. "He's been asking for a dog for months. Now, when he sees yours—"

"Can I have one just like him?" Nathan chirped as Dash scrambled onto the chair with him.

"See what I mean?"

"I know just where you can get one," I assured Linda. "There are several greyhound rescues with whom I can put you in touch. You couldn't ask for a better pet. Of course, I'd never encourage you if you weren't sure. Adopting a greyhound is commitment for the life of the dog."

"Shh…."

"Can we, Mom? Can we? Quinn, could you go with us and help us pick one out? The doctor says I'm doing really well and…"

"See what you've done?" Linda inquired cheerfully to the sound of Nathan's giggling as Dash helpfully washed his face. Then she winked at me and mouthed the words *we'll talk later.*

"Glad to help. Have you got anything cold to drink around here?"

"Freshly made lemonade and homemade cookies. Will that do?"

"Perfect." I sank down onto a chair near Nathan's. He and Dash were deep into some boy-dog conversation that only the two of them could decipher.

When she returned from the house with the lemonade and cookies, Linda sat down on a third chair and grinned at me with a smile of self-satisfaction that immediately made me suspicious.

"Why are you looking at me that way?" I took a swallow of the icy drink and felt it seep deliciously down my throat. "Like the cat that ate the canary?"

"I hear it went well at Jack Harmon's place. Ben told Nathan it was the best day he's had in a long time. 'Better than a baseball game,' he told Nate."

"Wow, and the Twins are winning right now, too." I hesitated before speaking again. "Is Jack overprotective with Ben?"

"Not really. Just careful. I would be, too, with a precious package like Ben. One day I overhead Ben tell Nathan about his exercises. 'Even when my body feels like lying down, I make my head tell it to stand up. If I don't, it will hurt even more tomorrow. Dad says I'm brave but I'm not. I just want to get better, that's all.' How sweet is that?"

"I wouldn't want to discourage a child like that, either."

"I told Jack it was impossible for you to do that." She eyed me speculatively. "I painted a picture of you that practically had a halo on it."

"I hope you tipped it sideways and made it tarnished." I leaned back in my chair and sipped from the sweating glass. "I can't work miracles, you know."

"If you can help and encourage Ben, his father will be forever grateful. You might even be responsible for some healing on Jack's part."

"What do you mean?"

"Because Emily is gone, she's become a bit of a saint in Jack's eyes. He's very loyal to her memory. He remembers all her good points and none of her imperfections."

"You said she was a wonderful person."

"She was. The best. But she was also the first to tell you her flaws. She was perfectly wonderful and perfectly human. She wouldn't want Jack to put her on a pedestal and keep her there. Life isn't a museum and Emily would want him to move on."

As I reached out and poured myself another glass of lemonade, Linda studied me slyly. "Jack's cute, isn't he?"

"Cute?"

"Okay, gorgeous. But I'm married. I'm not supposed to be looking."

"You aren't blind, either."

"I'd have to be, I suppose, not to see that Jack is incredible. He's as kind as he is good looking, too. I'm sorry he's had to suffer so much."

Linda looked pensive. "After his wife died, he turned off the fun, social part of his life to channel his energy into caring for Ben. Maybe, with your help, that will change."

"How would *I* be able to help? I'm hardly a social director." I stretched my legs as we talked and wriggled my toes. Ironically, during my last pedicure the stylist had painted tiny butterflies on my big toes. Butterflies. *Chrysalis*. Was this a new theme in my life or what?

"He'll have free time to bring some fun back into his life." Linda's tone changed, drawing my attention back to her. "Or you could be the fun. Maybe he'll ask you out."

"Linda!"

"You're both single, aren't you?"

"From what you've told me, it sounds like only one of us is."

"You may be right. In his mind, Jack is still very married."

"And that's a competition I'm not willing to fight."

"I suppose you're right. It's a shame, though. You would make a cute couple."

Nathan and Dash walked into the kitchen. "You should show your dog to Ben," he announced.

"Oh, I don't think so." Showing up on the Harmons' doorstep didn't sound like a good idea, especially after my conversation with Linda. I wouldn't want Jack to even think that I had interest in them beyond Ben's education.

"It's a great idea," Linda countered. "I'll put some

cookies in a container for you to take to them. A dog and cookies—what more could a little boy want?"

"That's not necessary."

"You don't have to stay. Show the child your dog and give him the cookies." Linda practically pushed me out the door.

Get it over with, I told myself as the cookies burned a hole in my hand. Dash and I were halfway up the walk when Jack and Ben rounded the house and stopped to stare at their visitors. We make quite a pair, Dash and I. We are both long, leggy and have slightly unusual looks that often make people stare.

Ben, eyes wide, moved toward Dash, but Jack put a hand on the boy's shoulder. "Does he bite?"

Ben squirmed away from his father. Ben looks as spindly and fragile as Dash, I realized, but Dash is *meant* to look that way and he, at least, is anything but fragile.

"Not unless you're a doggy treat.'

"Can I touch him?"

"Of course. If it's okay with your dad, that is."

And I thought this kid's eyes couldn't get any wider.

Ben reached out a tentative hand and stroked Dash's back. "He's so smooth!"

Jack, after eyeing Dash and seeing no danger, leaned against the wall, hands in his pockets, looking like a Ralph Lauren model on a break.

Even I, who am accustomed to being around good-looking men, find the way Jack carries himself with so much ease and grace enticing. A man at home in his own body and mind is very appealing. I spend too much time with models and aspiring actors who are always trying, because of the demands of their jobs, to be someone or something other than what they really are.

"Nice dog."

"He is," I agreed. "The best. We were out for a walk and ended up down the street." I thrust a package of cookies into his hand. "Linda sent these."

"She's taken us on board with her own family. We are very grateful. We've tried almost every bakery in the Cities and her cookies are still best. Would you like to come in? I know from experience that these are best served with cold milk."

Never let it be said I passed up a homemade cookie or, now that I'm here, a chance to visit with a charming man.

I followed him into the house. Ben insisted that Dash come inside, as well. We settled at the kitchen table which, today, was flour-free. The volcano sat unfinished on the counter.

Ben's gaze traveled with mine toward the project. "It's dry enough to put another coat on now, Dad says. We're going to do it this afternoon." He looked at me shyly through his eyelashes. "Could you help?"

"Ben, that's not why Ms. Hunter came—"

"It's okay. I don't mind."

Frankly, I dumbfounded myself with the answer.

"Ben, she has her dog with her," Jack said mildly, allowing me another chance to renege on my answer.

"He can sit on the floor right by me, just like he's doing now." Ben pointed a finger at Dash who was poised like a statue at his feet. Dash looked frozen in time, like a drawing of the ancient Egyptians at the pyramids.

Jack looked helplessly at me. "You don't have to, you know."

"I know, but I will. I'm particularly fond of building volcanoes."

"Suit yourself." He grinned and shook his head. "All I can guarantee you is a big mess."

He had that right.

A half hour later I touched my gluey finger to what should be the crest of the mountain. "I think we need a little more height on this side."

"Here it comes." Jack draped a layer of the *papier mâché* where I pointed and his palm brushed the top of my hand.

A person wouldn't think that two hands, couched in *papier mâché,* could even feel each other, but the pressure of Jack's touch startled me. Although we'd shaken hands before, this felt different, oddly intimate, as we worked together for his son. His arm brushed mine as we navigated around the table and the encounter left me slightly shaken.

It wasn't until we were almost done positioning soggy paper onto the lump Ben fondly called a volcano that we realized that somewhere in the process Ben and Dash had escaped the kitchen. We could hear the murmur of the television in the other room. Suddenly Jack's hand touched mine again in the slick wet goo and a tingle shot up my arm.

"When did Ben and the dog sneak off?" Jack asked.

"And why didn't we notice it? Talk about adults being overinvolved in children's projects." My voice was a little shaky, but he didn't seem to notice. "But it's done. All Ben has to do now is wait for it to dry, paint and decorate it with stones."

Jack handed me a damp towel and I wiped my hands. Then he nodded at the doorway to the family room. Ben and Dash were sound asleep on the couch, entwined in a pretzellike configuration.

"I hope you don't mind animals on your furniture. Dash does it at home so I'm sure he thinks it's okay here. I can get him off."

Jack stopped me as I stepped forward. "I think he was invited. Ben's content and that's what counts."

He washed his hands beneath the faucet. Nice, strong, firm and well-manicured hands that usually did not have glue under the nails. "How about I brew some coffee to go with the rest of those cookies?"

"I shouldn't…" Even though I wanted to.

"Why not?" He looked at me, his eyes warm as melted *chocolate* and the smile lines at the corners crinkling agreeably.

"I didn't mean to intrude on your day."

"You aren't. The volcano is done. The least I can do is give you a cup of coffee in payment."

Okay, so I'm weak-willed and a sucker for coffee and chocolate…chocolate-colored eyes.

Chapter Ten

Jack moved easily around the kitchen, trim hipped, wide-shouldered and oozing testosterone. I couldn't help but stare. He expertly ground coffee beans, arranged Linda's cookies on a plate and put it on a tray with coffee cups. Each time he turned my way, he would smile at me and a slash of something too masculine to be called dimples flashed in his cheeks.

As I watched Jack brew coffee I realized that I was probably enjoying this too much. Can I help it that I like watching this man who obviously knows his way around a kitchen?

Jack lifted the lid on a Crock-Pot and savory fumes wafted through the air. Beef bourguignonne. Could it be?

"It smells wonderful. Do you cook a lot?"

He looked sheepish. "I owe all my gourmet recipes to the Food Channel. It's the closest thing I can find to having someone take me by the hand and show me how something is done." He shuffled his feet and, for a split second, looked exactly like his ten-year-old son. "I tape shows so I can go back and rewatch them. It's probably ridiculous sounding, but Ben and I eat better."

His face clouded. "Emily was a wonderful cook."

"Linda said your wife was a wonderful person. I'm sorry for your loss—and Ben's."

Jack nodded bleakly. "We met in college through mutual friends, but it wasn't until later that we started to date. We had a lot going on in our lives—grad school, travel, volunteer stuff. We both wanted to drink as deeply as we could of life, I guess. Looking back, I'm glad we got the opportunity to do so—especially Emily."

I could see him turning inward, viewing a private video taken years before.

"Emily was a travel journalist. Sometimes I teased her that she was more comfortable on a plane than in our living room. That stopped when Ben came along. Everything lost its significance in comparison to him."

Jack set a creamer on the table and poured coffee into a cup. His fingers and mine touched as I took it.

"Emily sounds like quite a woman. Tell me more about her."

I'm not the prying sort, but it seemed important to understand the woman my new student and his father had loved.

Jack looked surprised but pleased. "I don't want to bore you."

"You won't."

"Em was beautiful. Ben got his blue eyes and dark gold hair from her. Little kids at kindergarten used to ask Ben if his mommy was a movie star."

I tried to imagine Ben's eyes and hair on that of a beautiful woman. It wasn't difficult.

"Ben always told them no, she wasn't a movie star but that she was better—she was a 'Mommy Star.'" Jack turned his face away momentarily, as if he didn't want me to see the pain there. "One of the first things Ben asked after Em died was 'Is she really a Mommy Star now?'"

I had invaded deeply private territory.

"Emily had a very deep faith in God. I told Ben that whatever she's doing now, she is happier than she's ever been before. Ben's okay with that and I am, too. We're just lonesome for her, that's all." Then he shook himself like Dash does after being out in the rain. "But you don't want to hear about this."

Oh, I don't know about that. My curiosity was stirred. "What did she and Ben enjoy doing together?"

He appeared surprised at the question but recovered quickly.

"Cook, of course. Swim. Go fishing. She always thought of ways to keep him busy with things that he was capable of doing. They played games for hours on end and read books together. If Ben had said he wanted to take up stamp collecting or sky-diving, she would have made it happen."

"She sounds like fun."

"She was. Her laughter could fill an entire room…." Jack bowed his head.

It took him some moments to recover, but when he lifted his head he was smiling ruefully. "I really gave you an earful, didn't I? You should be more careful. I could have bored you to death. You are much too good a listener."

"I was never in danger, thank you very much. I'm in awe of that kind of love."

Jack poured himself coffee and came to sit across from me at the table. "Me, too. I never thought it would happen for me. That, more than anything, is why I'll never marry again. I know I couldn't be that lucky twice in my life."

I opened my mouth to speak and then snapped it shut.

"I started with the best. There's no way to improve on that."

He's practically sanctified that woman. I hear Linda's words in my head, ones she confided to me in our discussion about Jack.

Linda had certainly pegged that right.

Then some life came back into his features. "Emily left us a lot of wonderful gifts and memories, but the best gift of all she gave to Ben."

"What's that?"

"His spirit. Ben is all about laughter, about trust and about possibilities. In spite of his pain, he never gives in to it. He's a fighter, determined as Napoleon Bonaparte in his march across Europe and relentless as an ocean tide. He just never quits." Awe tinged Jack's voice. "Remarkable."

"And that was his mother's spirit, too?" No wonder Jack felt he'd never be quite whole again.

"It was, but I believe Ben is even…more so. Of course, Ben had an added element in his equation. My wife had to come to grips with her own mortality. She had to surrender everything to God and trust Him to get her through what was ahead of her."

"And little Ben watched."

"Like a hawk. He wouldn't leave her side when the pastor came from the church or when friends came to pray.

"When she died, it was Ben who was the rock in the family. He was calm and confident, even peaceful. He kept reminding the rest of us that his mother was fine, that she was happy. 'We're just crying for ourselves, you know,' he told his grandmother. 'Mom wouldn't like that. She never liked it when one of us was unhappy.'"

My heart lodged itself in my throat.

"When his grandmother asked him how he became so wise," Jack recalled, "Ben grinned at her said, 'Me and Mom talked to God about it. He promised and we believe Him.'"

"So you see—" Jack looked at me with sharp, intelligent eyes "—I am motivated to do any- and everything I can for Ben. He's my role model, my hero and—" there was a catch in his voice "—my terribly vulnerable little boy."

And Jack had entrusted me his precious jewel of a child to me.

Lord, help me not to let this pair down!

At that moment Ben and Dash entered the room. Ben had his hand on Dash's collar. It was not necessary, of course. Dash would have followed him anywhere.

"What are you doing, Dad?"

"Quinn and I are having coffee."

"Can Dash and I have some of the cookies?"

"You can. Dash has his own diet."

Ben eyed his father, then me. "Are you taking today off?"

Odd question for a child.

"I'm working at home today, Ben," Jack said.

Ben turned to me. "He works too much. Sometimes I worry about him."

I blinked, startled. He sounded more like Jack's father than his son.

Jack chuckled and ruffled Ben's hair. "Go eat your cookies, old man. And remember, I'm the father, not you."

When they were gone, Jack sank into a chair with a sigh. "We're a pair, aren't we? I worry about him and he worries about me. We need more fun in our lives."

Although I protested, Jack insisted on driving me and Dash back to my place.

"We managed to get here, there'll be no trouble going home. Honestly."

"It's the 'you' part of the equation that I'm concerned about. That dog of yours could run into tomorrow."

Dash, in the backseat, pricked his ears, sensing that he was the topic of conversation.

"Well, I did lose some of my energy while I was sitting down." I relaxed into the passenger seat. "I haven't been running as regularly as I should."

"Besides," Ben piped up from the back where he was strapped into a seat belt with Dash's paws across his lap, "I want to see where you live."

"It's nothing special. It's a very old house, in fact. My grandparents lived there."

"Cool." Ben stared out the window as Jack turned the car off France Avenue and he started to see the cozy stucco bungalows that signaled my neighborhood. Children played hopscotch on the sidewalk and a boy tossed a Frisbee to a black Lab that caught it midair. "It looks like a storybook house."

It does, actually. Maggie, skilled gardener that she is, works her heart out on our lawn and landscaping. There's never a month in the summer that a new set of plants aren't blooming as others fade back. The yard is always a riot of color. Between my birdbaths and feeders and her butterfly gardens and seed catalogue spending sprees, the only thing missing from the yard is Bambi sniffing a flower.

"Look! There's another Dash!" Ben pointed toward my front step and Dash scrambled up to see what was going on. His tail began to thump wildly.

"Actually, that is Flash, my friend's dog. We adopted Flash and Dash at the same time."

Jack pulled to a stop and when I opened the door, Dash scrambled past me for a giddy meeting with his friend.

"Would you like to come in?" I wasn't sure if I wanted Jack to say yes or no. I knew Pete would give him a once-over, if not the third degree.

"I'd like a rain check." Jack leaned forward. "And thanks for all the help."

"Call me anytime." That sounded a little coy, but I doubt Jack heard me say it. Ben was too busy demanding to know when "another time" would be and if they could come back tomorrow.

I watched them drive off with mixed emotions. Affection, respect, anticipation and strangely, a little sadness. I like Jack and respect the way he's raising his son. Yet no matter how long we work together for Ben's benefit, I already know that Jack Harmon will always be remote and inaccessible as anything more than a friend, living his life in the past with a woman who can't love him back.

Chapter Eleven

I walked through the kitchen door to discover Maggie and Pete at the kitchen table sharing a pizza and a liter of diet soda. Dash and Flash were already at Pete's side watching the pizza Pete was holding, as if it was a mechanical rabbit at the track.

"You're home!" I threw out my arms to hug Maggie. "How are you, sweetie?"

She was wearing her favorite T-shirt, one Pete had given her during a previous dustup with her sisters. I Can't Remember If I'm The Good Sister Or The Evil One. Her cheeks were a hint rounder than they had been when she left, even though she'd been at her mother's only a few days. Maggie's angular features were always softened by a couple extra pounds. Frankly, she looked fabulous.

When I get upset, I go for comfort food. Mashed potatoes three times a day is good enough for me. When Maggie is distressed, however, she turns into a garbage disposal, downing everything that comes her way. That also explained the three-meat pizza with extra cheese.

"I am so glad to see you!" I scrunched her cheeks between the palms of my hands. "I've missed you."

"Glad someone has."

"Hey, what about me?" Pete yelped through a mouthful of pepperoni. "I missed you, too!"

Dash woofed in agreement.

"Not feeling much better, huh?" I grabbed a slice of pizza and joined them at the table.

"I thought I was. Then I walked into the house and saw the cashmere throw on the couch that Randy gave me. I went into the bathroom and what was on the counter? Euphoria. Randy's favorite perfume. When I picked up my mail, there was a receipt for a pair of tickets I'd ordered so we could see the *Birth of Broadway* concert. He's everywhere I turn."

Pete, being very guylike, volunteered. "I like the Minnesota Orchestra. I'll go with you, Maggie."

"I don't think that's the problem." I helped myself to soda. "You're all wrong for the job."

"And Randy is all right? Ha!" He waved the pizza so little red pepper flakes scattered across the table.

"Oh, I'll be okay—someday," Maggie said gloomily. "My mother keeps saying, there are other fish in the sea." She stared into the bottom of her half-empty glass of soda. "Sad to say, most of them are carp."

"Fortunately we don't have monkfish here." I'd watched my mother prepare a monkfish once. It was so ugly that I'd dreamed about it living under the kitchen sink for months and refused to eat any seafood except fish sticks.

"Speaking as a very handsome walleye or perhaps a rainbow trout," Pete interjected, "I can guarantee there are more good fish in the sea than you might imagine. We're just a little leery of being caught."

"Terrific. That leaves me with a choice of bottom-feeders, right?"

"Not if you use the right bait."

Pete meant it playfully, but Maggie's response was anything but. She burst into tears.

"That's the whole problem, isn't it? I'm lousy bait!"

We both stared at her as if she'd caught a fish hook in her brain. "What?"

"There's something wrong with me—otherwise Randy wouldn't have left."

"You've broken up with guys, too, you know."

"Sure. Because there's something about them I don't like—they eat with their mouths open, are rude to waitresses or poor tippers…"

"We're swimming in shallow water here," Pete muttered, casting the fish metaphor out far too long.

"Why do you want a man who doesn't want you?" I didn't mean to be harsh, but Maggie has to get over the idea that if she were prettier, better dressed or more obliging, Randy might have stayed.

"You just don't get it. You are always the dumper, not the dumpee!" She flounced into her room and slammed the door.

Pete and I stared at each other. Dumper and dumpee? Now what?

Typical Americans that we are, we turned on the television and watched a couple shop for a new home and a frenetic designer try to remake someone's home in twelve hours. Finally, when our eyes were beginning to glaze over, Pete mumbled, "I've got Rollerblades in my car."

"You're tired of HGTV?"

"These people are too happy. They're getting on my nerves."

"Then let's make the boys smile instead."

The boys—Dash and Flash—were downright delirious as Pete and I let them race us down the street and around the walking trails in the park. We must look a sight when we do it—intense, loping dogs pulling their terrified old-enough-to-know-better owners on Rollerblades—a recipe for disaster if there ever was one.

We've wiped out a time or two, Dash and I. And once Flash dragged Pete through a break in the sidewalk that left him sprawled on the ground with so much skin scraped off his cheek and arm that he ended up in the E.R. But we still do it. It's our mild way of living on the edge.

Pete tipped his head toward Maggie's door before he headed home. "Are you two going to be okay?"

"Of course. Maggie and I are practically sisters. She trusts me to tell her the truth even when she doesn't want to hear it. That's part of our deal."

"I'm glad she has the health-club job coming up soon. That will distract her. She's really excited about it."

"Are you shooting it?"

"I am. I haven't heard anything about it lately so I assume everything is on schedule."

I felt the pressure lift in my chest. "Good. She needs a distraction."

"And someone fawning over her," Pete added grimly. "She acts like she's only half a person without a man. When will that girl wake up and smell the coffee?"

Not until tomorrow morning apparently, when the coffeepot's automatic brewer engages, for when I went to pray with Maggie, I found her sound asleep on her bed. I covered her with a downy comforter, then went to my room to do some serious praying on my own.

"What's this?" Maggie waved a piece of paper under my nose when I walked into the kitchen the next morning. Her hair was sleep-mussed and sometime in the night she had awakened and changed into a pair of boxer shorts and an oversized T-shirt.

On a napkin I had doodled the word *Chrysalis* with a downward smiley face.

"Just scribbling. It's nothing."

Frank had called yesterday with dual purposes. The first was to convince me that I'd be passing up a great thing if I didn't take this job with his company. The second was to invite me out to dinner to help me change my mind.

That's like being invited out by a cannibal for "a little bite to eat." He'd pressured me just enough to make me uneasy. Fortunately I was already busy.

"Just a job I turned down."

Her head snapped up sharply. "Oh?"

"Hostess for a reality show, makeovers with a twist." I summed it up as succinctly as I could.

She nodded absently. "Hostess, huh? Is the pay good?"

She studied herself in the reflection from the toaster, a replica of the kind that had been in my mother's kitchen when I was growing up. "I suppose I'd better get to Pete's and find out what he knows about our shoot." She put her hand on her stomach. "I'm getting fluttery just thinking about it. I am so grateful to have this job to take my mind off things.

"I'm sorry about last night." Her eyes welled with tears. "You told me the truth and I took it badly. I should be grateful. You are one of the few people in the world I can count on for unvarnished honesty and you're right. I *don't* want a man who doesn't want me."

She hugged me before heading for her room. "I'd better get ready. Pete's probably waiting for me."

After she'd gone, I lingered at the table so long that Dash lay down across my feet and fell asleep.

Lord, I don't know what it's going to take, but please help Maggie start depending on You for her worth and value.

My thoughts whirled with all that had been going on in the past few days.

And give me what I need to be the best tutor and friend I can to little Ben Harmon. What a bright light he is. And help his father, Jack. Ease his pain, as well. Only You know what's supposed to happen next, but I ask that I be in the center of Your will, no matter what it is. Amen.

Because I had a few hours to waste, I indulged myself in my secret pleasure, shopping.

Not for myself, of course. I'm a clotheshorse who doesn't care that much for clothes. I love to shop for babies.

I find that little pink dresses with ruffles, soft, cottony blankets and blue-and-white sweatshirts with tiny embroidered baseballs and bats are irresistible. Baby soap is my favorite scent and it's my other passion to find unique diaper pins and soft washcloths. I buy them by the shopping cartful with only one reservation. They have to be on sale. Cheap. Because I want to buy in quantity. Obscene quantities, actually.

I am a baby-clothes freak and the layette ladies at church love me for it.

This passion started for me as a child not satisfied with the bits of money I put into the offering plate on Sunday. I asked my mother if there was anything a little kid could do to help out at church. I didn't know how to quilt or cook and was too young to have a job and donate money.

My mother, wise woman that she is, came up with the idea of contributing to the layettes the church ladies were making for new mothers. First she brought home bolts of soft flannel fabric and taught me how to cut blanket- and diaper-sized pieces and zigzag the edges. After I had made stacks of both, she took me to the dollar store and gave me orders to buy as much baby soap and as many diaper pins as I could with the money. Soon I added my own babysitting wages to the pot. By the time I was in high school, I had all my friends shopping with me and our church was sending layettes not to just one missionary hospital but several. In college I was called "The Baby Lady" which took some explaining to the uninitiated—especially guys who wanted to date me.

I still indulge myself in my vision—that every new mother have something new for her baby no matter what her standing in life or country of origin. Pete says I'm changing the world, one mama and baby at a time. There are worse hobbies, I guess.

Anyway, by the time I hit a sale on flannel at the local discount store, stocked up on tiny T-shirts and sleepers at seventy percent off and bought odds and ends of baby yarn to knit a couple sweaters, I was feeling better about everything. So good, in fact, that I stopped at Starbucks for an infusion of caffeine and a chance to read the newspaper uninterrupted.

I'd been home only five minutes when my cell phone rang.

Pete's strangled voice whispered across the line.

"Get over here, Quinn. *Now.*"

Chapter Twelve

Pete doesn't panic. Pete frets, stews, mulls, ponders, fusses and fumes, but he doesn't panic. Not even when Flash ate a canister of film from Pete's largest-paying-ever shoot. Fortunately, everything, as Pete put it, "came out just fine."

I grabbed my purse and headed for the door. "Dash, come. Ride."

He went from comatose to alert in a nanosecond. *Ride* is one of Dash's favorite words, right up there with *eat* and *walk*. He does *fetch, heel* and *stay* without enthusiasm. *Roll over* insults him, but he does it out of deference to me. He views me as the pleasant but rather unenlightened member of his pack. I am not alpha dog. I may be omega dog in Dash's eyes.

Dash hopped into the front seat and waited for me to buckle his doggy seat belt. I was on the road within five minutes of Pete's call.

Pete's studio is in the area of 50th Street and France

Avenue and it took me only a few minutes to get to Images. As I walked from the parking ramp I ignored all the small, tempting shops including a brand-new chocolateria that had just opened in the storefront next to his, although I did take several deep breaths as I went by. Maggie's Triumph was parallel parked in front of the studio. Pete currently has his black-and-white photography on display in the reception area of the studio. Six-foot-high pictures of body parts—a foot and ankle in a Manolo Blahnik, a wrist draped in charm bracelets and a closed eye lined with kohl and fringed with impossibly long lashes—greeted me. I liked it better when Pete was in his "baby stage" and the walls were lined with cherubic babies wearing nothing but a smile.

Everyone, including Flash and Dash, loves having Pete take their picture. They like it because he keeps them alert and attentive with doggy treats. I have more portraits of Dash in the house than I do of my family. Of course, Dash is the only one actually willing to sit still long enough to make it happen.

The reception area of the studio was empty except for Flash who, upon seeing Dash, wagged from the tip of his tail to the top of his head. I left them to perform their doggy hellos and headed for the break room.

All was quiet. Maggie was seated at Pete's small retro laminate-topped table holding a mug of coffee in both hands. She stared trancelike out the back window onto the alley at a large Dumpster ready to be emptied.

Pete made pointing motions toward Maggie and a dramatic slitting motion across his neck.

She wants to kill herself? I mouthed.

Pete wagged his head in the negative. Then he began miming himself at a photo shoot, taking pictures.

"She wants to kill you?"

"Of course not!" he blurted aloud. Maggie never even flinched. She simply continued to grip her mug and stare out the window.

"Mags, Quinn is here. We'll go into the studio and I'll tell her what's coming down. We'll be right back."

Maggie never acknowledged his words.

"What on earth…"

"I thought you'd never get here," Pete blurted. "I don't know what to do. The general manager from the fitness club's corporate office called me to say that there'd been a 'change in plans.' They took another look at the direction of their advertising and decided to move away from images of people in their ads. They've developed a new logo and plan to use photos of their facilities in their advertising."

My stomach fluttered uneasily.

"Now they want me to go to their gyms and do photo shoots of the buildings and a series on the machines. I asked what would happen to the model they'd hired."

The flutter became a jackhammer in my gut.

"The general manager said, as casually as can be, that she'd been 'cut loose.' They'd sent her a registered letter notifying her that she wouldn't be needed."

"Maggie…"

"I didn't know if I should tell her." Pete shifted restlessly, hands in his pockets, anxiety writen all over his face. "Then I imagined her getting the letter and decided to try to soften the blow." He nodded toward the break room. "A big help that was. Look at her."

"What did you tell her?"

"Pretty much what I just told you. I didn't say she would be 'cut loose' as they so crassly put it, but Maggie is good at reading between the lines." Pete looked so miserable that my heart went out to him. "She usually reads too much into things but this time, she was right on the money."

"What did she say?"

"'I'm being replaced by a row of elliptical trainers and rowing machines?'" Pete spread his hands helplessly. "What could I say to that?"

"You could have said 'yes.'"

Maggie stood in the doorway of the break room. Neither Pete nor I knew how long she'd been there or how much she had heard.

She moved gracefully, like a wraith, across the hardwood floor to us. "It wasn't your fault. You were trying to protect me."

"It wasn't anybody's fault, especially not yours. In our business these things happen…."

Maggie shook her head emphatically. "I don't believe that."

"The company had no business hiring people for a concept they weren't totally committed to," I blustered, feeling both furious and frustrated.

"Don't you see? I'm the one who failed them. If I'd been right—thinner, more attractive, the exact person they wanted on their billboards—they would have been loyal to me."

"Maggie," Pete said impatiently, "corporations change their minds all the time about how they want to be perceived. It's not about a single person and it's certainly not about you. It was a company decision."

"Why didn't they just *try* me first?" she murmured, more to herself than to us. "I could have been anything they wanted—hip, buff, come-hither. I'd make myself into exactly what they wanted."

"Make yourself into whatever they wanted?" Pete echoed incredulously. "Why would you do that?"

"To get the job, of course."

She looked so fragile and lost as she said it that tears came to my eyes.

"Oh, Maggie, I know…"

"You can't know what it's like, Quinn. Everyone wants to hire you!"

Pete took up my case. "People who want dark-haired models with exotic features don't call Quinn. She's Scandinavian as fish balls in white gravy, lefse and King Harald! No matter what she did, she couldn't—wouldn't—look like you."

"You can talk all you want, but I don't believe it. If I were different I know I would have kept this job."

"Do you remodel your house every time your mood changes? Do you paint your car to match your nail polish? Come on, Maggie, get real! You can't change who you are for others. Be who you are and let the right ones come to you!"

We might as well have been talking to one of Pete's backdrops. Maggie ignored everything we said.

She didn't speak when she arrived at home. Nor did

she murmur a word when she took the official-looking letter from the fitness club out of the mailbox. She threw it into the garbage, walked into her room, closed the door firmly and locked it.

The finality of her movements told me that, no matter how much I wanted to talk about this, the matter was not up for discussion.

Knowing Maggie was locked in her bedroom grieving made it impossible for me to focus on lesson plans. Ready for a distraction, I was more than a little relieved when my doorbell rang.

The last people I expected to see were Jack and Ben Harmon framed in the doorway. Jack looked embarrassed and uncomfortable, but Ben was obviously elated to be here.

"I told him it wasn't appropriate to drop in on you." Jack's tone was apologetic.

"I knew you wouldn't mind," Ben said, beaming at me like a halogen flashlight. Just because you are my teacher doesn't mean you can't be my friend, too. Right?"

"He wouldn't listen…."

"Dad said this was a 'business arrangement,' but I'm not a business and you're not an arrangement," Ben insisted. "Besides, you are the only one I want to go to the Science Museum with me. They've got this really cool show on now. Did you know that Pluto isn't a planet, anymore? And they have moon rocks and meteorites. My friend Nathan says you know a lot about outer space. Do you really think the dinosaurs died because…" Ben paused to take a breath. "Want to come?"

"She isn't going to be interested, Ben." Jack put a

comforting hand on his son's shoulder as if to brace him for a disappointment.

I looked at the closed door that separated Maggie and me. She would probably sleep a long time. A person simply can't cry as hard and long as she had without becoming exhausted.

"You can't just drop in on people and assume they have time for you, Ben," Jack continued.

"Sometimes you can."

Jack's head jerked up as if he hadn't heard me correctly.

"You will?" Ben squealed. "You'll come?"

I bent to look Ben straight in the baby blues. "Your Dad is right. Call ahead and make plans next time, but today I would like to get out of the house. I was planning to go to that exhibit, anyway, so there's no time like the present."

Ben screwed his head around to look triumphantly at his dad. "See? I told you she'd go."

Jack's face cleared and his dark eyes lit in his tanned face. It made him look impossibly young and handsome. "And I thought I knew how the world worked."

"Let me write a note to my roommate so she knows where I've gone when she wakes up. I'll take my car and follow you to St. Paul."

"That wrecks all the fun!" Ben protested. He turned again to his befuddled father. "We'll bring her home whenever she wants, won't we, Dad?"

Jack gave up the battle. "Sure. Why not?"

"You don't have to…"

Then Jack's face creased into a smile and I saw where Ben got all that irresistible charm. "But we *want* to. Please?"

I wrote Maggie a note, grabbed a sweater and followed them to Jack's van. It looked like a home away from home, with a DVD player, movies, games and books scattered about the backseat, as well as a gym bag, tennis racquet and golf shoes. There was a twelve-pack of soda and a bag of tortilla chips piled on top of undelivered dry cleaning. Yes, indeed, the Harmon vehicle was definitely a man's domain.

But far be it from me to say I don't like a little testosterone in the mix. Ben and I sat in the backseat discussing black holes, dinosaurs, volcanoes and the merits of really goopy mud while Jack sat in front and drove. It must have looked like a cozy family scene to passersby when we emptied out of the van.

Looks can be deceiving.

Ben was so impatient that he bounced and spun on his tiptoes and made impatient noises until we were ready to go inside.

To see the familiar through new eyes, join a small boy with an inquiring mind in a museum.

"Why are rocks colored?"

"Where does wind start?"

"Do snakes have good eyesight?"

"Do fish have taste buds?"

"Do hummingbirds really hum?"

Jack put his hand on my arm and we hung back as Ben raced ahead to examine the towboat in the Mississippi River Gallery.

"Is your head starting to ache? One more question and my eyeballs will start spinning in my head."

"Lively curiosity, that's all. I enjoy seeing that in a

child." The feel of his touch on my arm was both tender and caring. I might not have noticed if it weren't for the fact that Jack is normally so restrained. His son, on the other hand, throws his arms around my waist whenever the impulse strikes him. Missing his mother? I wondered. Craving maternal touch?

I don't believe Jack is unaffectionate or aloof. Just the opposite, in fact. He is holding his life together with sheer willpower. When Ben wished aloud that his mother could play with him in the experiment gallery, I'd felt Jack's entire body stiffen, bracing himself against a wave of pain.

Linda had warned me that Jack has no time for relationships with women. It's no wonder. Lowering his guard against emotional contact might break down the fragile walls that keep him together.

How must it be to have experienced a love like Jack and Emily's? I can't imagine it yet, but I'm waiting, holding out for the transcendent love they had.

Ben appeared to approve of his father and I walking together as we strolled through the museum. Each time he looked back to see where we were, he smiled broadly. After nearly two hours, I began to suspect that he was dallying and dragging out this afternoon for reasons of his own.

"I really should be getting home—"

Ben cut me off. "I want to look at the Rapetosaurus again."

So we trudged off to see the fascinating long-necked sauropod with its long thin teeth, elongated neck and slender tail.

Ben took me by the hand and tugged at it until I bent down so he could look directly into my eyes. His gaze was intent, mesmerizing. "Can we go to the 3-D cinema before we go? I really want to see the show. Nathan hasn't seen it yet and I want to beat him to it. Okay?"

I hesitated and Jack hastened to say, "It's totally up to you. You told us you wanted to be home early."

At that moment my phone rang. It was Pete.

"Just thought you might want to know that Maggie is with me. You don't have to hurry home."

"Are you sure?"

"We're taking a walk to clear our heads. Take your time. Have fun."

I closed my phone and looked at Ben. "Let's go."

He let out an earsplitting whistle, grabbed my hand and tugged me toward the theater.

We scooted into our seats, with Ben between us, but at the last moment Ben wormed his way over his father's lap, leaving me to move next to Jack. As the theater darkened I was aware of Jack's firm body next to mine, radiating heat in the large, chilly room.

Ben scuffled and leaned toward his father.

"Dad, why don't you hold her hand?" he whispered just loud enough so that I couldn't ignore it. "It's okay."

Jack stiffened and pulled his body inward like a black hole caving in on itself.

"Watch the movie, Ben." His voice was controlled but cracked a little as he added, "I love you, buddy, don't worry about me."

I don't remember a single thing we watched in the cinema. All I could think of was Ben observing and caring for his father, offering him permission to move ahead with his life. And then there was Jack, who understood but simply couldn't budge from the emotional Antarctica in which he was trapped.

Chapter Thirteen

Jack and I did not look at each other as we exited the cinema. The brightness outside the theater left us blinking and shielding our eyes. It also gave us an excuse not to connect over Ben's dark blond head.

Although Jack and I were uncomfortable over Ben's expressed permission for us to hold hands, Ben seemed to have forgotten all about it.

"I want to go to the Explore Store," he chirped. "There are very cool things in there."

Depleted of energy to stem this boy's tide, Jack acquiesced. "Go ahead. Quinn and I will find coffee and wait for you outside the store by that small table in the corner."

"Can I have some money, Dad?"

Jack opened his billfold and counted out dollar bills. "Don't waste it."

"Nope." And Ben was off like a shot.

"I expected Ben to tire first." I kicked off my shoes

and breathed a sigh of relief. "He's the one with a condition, not me."

"The child can run on vapors," Jack said with a chuckle.

"I never realized how pleasant a day at the museum could be," I told Jack when he returned with a latte for me. "He is going to be a challenge and a delight to work with."

"You mean you still want to? I thought that today might scare you off." Jack looked at me with an affectionate expression tinged with a hint of laughter. "You may run away, screaming at the top of your lungs now if you wish."

"You've got to give me—and Ben—more credit than that!"

"Sorry about—"

I held up my index finger to shush him. I didn't mean to touch his lips, but there it was. They were warm and dry against my skin. I pulled away quickly. "Nothing, absolutely *nothing* to be sorry about. I had a wonderful time today. Truly."

"Me, too." A smile broke across his face like the sun chasing away the clouds. "Thanks for that, Quinn."

"Anytime." It astonished me how much I meant it. *Anytime!*

We sat back to enjoy our coffee, and Maggie's problems flooded back to me.

"You're preoccupied," Jack commented. "Something on your mind? Good ideas for harnessing my son's curiosity, I hope."

"I wish it were that easy."

Jack appeared to be contemplating my inner weather, which was, at the moment, stormy. "Want to talk about it?"

"I don't want to bother you with my personal problems."

His dark eyes, fringed with long dusky lashes were kind. He was so close that I could see tiny smile lines around his eyes in his tanned face. There wasn't an ounce of extra fat on Jack's lean frame, but he looked so solid and so real…and trustworthy.

"I'm a good listener."

"I'm sure you are."

"Ben is going to be gone at least half an hour. He inherited his mother's shopping genes. He has to examine everything in the store before he'll buy anything. Unless you have a burning desire to rehash what we've seen today, we've got the time."

It was tempting. As an objective listener, perhaps he could come up with an idea to help Maggie, something that Pete and I had missed.

"Tell me to stop if you get bored, okay?"

"I'm not too worried." His expression softened. "I know how it is not to have a sounding board. It can be a lonely place."

He knows lonely only too well.

"My friend and roomate Maggie and I are both models. Unfortunately, Maggie isn't cut out for the business. She takes it personally when she doesn't get a job. She's convinced herself that if *she* were different she would get more jobs. Her self-esteem is about this big." I held my index finger and thumb a quarter inch apart.

He listened intently as I told him about the health club, its decision to change its image and Maggie's crushing disappointment.

"She's scaring my friend Pete and me. We can't cajole her out of this destructive mood she's in. I'm sure she's falling into depression, but she won't admit that."

His eyes were compassionate and kind, as if he could feel Maggie's pain. "I didn't realize how difficult it might be to be in your profession."

"My temporary profession," I corrected. "I'm a teacher first and foremost. Modeling pays the bills so I can do more of what I want."

"Teaching?"

I realized that our index fingers were in such close proximity that they were nearly touching and that a little spark seemed to be traveling back and forth between them like the pull of two magnets being held apart.

I drew my attention away from my hand and back to Jack's face. "Tutoring. I'm not sure anyone understands the draw or the affection I feel for my students. Sometimes even I don't get it. I just accept that God made me a teacher to my core. To ignore that would be to disregard my calling and the children whose lives He wants me to touch."

He nodded as if he approved of my answer. "But back to your friend."

"Maggie has been counting on that contract. It was the one thing she felt she had going for her." Jack listened with his entire body, as if the story I told was the most important thing on earth.

"Her boyfriend left her a few days ago and she's devastated. Today she got the word that she'd been dropped from the health-club account."

"Ouch."

"No kidding. That's why I don't dare say much about an offer I just received. I'm turning it down, anyway, and I don't want to make her feel worse than she already does."

"What's the offer?"

Impulsively, I put my hand on top of his as it rested on the table. His hand was strong, sinewy and warm to the touch. His smooth skin felt silken beneath my palm. His eyes, when he looked at me were so tender that my tongue and my brain tangled like that lump of gold chains in my jewelry box that I've never been able to separate.

"Your new job?" he prodded gently.

"Not my new job, my new job *offer*," I corrected. "It's a reality-television show."

I took a breath and plunged in, blathering about everything from cocoon to emergence.

"Is it so bad, really? The contestants know what they're in for. Maybe it's their one and only chance to have their ears lowered or get rid of that nose of Aunt Brunhild's that they inherited."

I was surprised at his perspective. "But it's such a slippery slope to put people on and a terrible message to convey. You're special when you are beautiful and not so special if you aren't. Beauty is transitory and short-lived. We both know that. An accident, an illness, great unhappiness…" His expression tightened and I realized he was thinking of his wife. "All those things can erase the physical beauty we strive for. Then what? Does it mean someone isn't important because men don't turn their heads or women don't gawk enviously when she walks by?"

He frowned, rolling this information around in his

head like so many rocks in a tumbler. "I see what you mean." His engaging smile tipped one corner of his mouth. "I'm eternally grateful that people don't judge me by my looks alone."

Even though Jack is incredible looking, his greatest charm and appeal are still in the way he interacts with his son, the dignity with which he bears his loss and the twinkle that's never far from his eyes even when the conversation is uncomfortably serious—like now.

"There's a verse in Proverbs that keeps looping through my thoughts. When pride comes, disgrace comes. Wisdom is with the humble—something like that. That's why every alarm bell goes off and every red flag starts to wave for me when I think about *Chrysalis.*"

Jack opened a chocolate-chip-macadamia-nut cookie the size of a salad plate, broke it and handed half to me.

"It is easy to get wrapped up in staying beautiful and become a slave to the latest wrinkle cream or lip plumper."

"They have lip *plumbers* now?" He looked incredulous.

"Not 'plumbers,' *plumpers*... Oh, never mind." I grinned. "It just shows that you'll never be a part of the better-living-through-cosmetics-and-plastic-surgery crowd."

"I certainly hope not." He smiled and it was as if I saw Ben beaming at me with pure enjoyment in his eyes. It was a look I could easily get used to.

"So this show says that beauty is all important and that if you've got it, flaunt it. And that rubs you the wrong way because of James 4:6?"

"You know that verse?"

"My wife was a very strong Christian and she nurtured my faith, as well. Anytime anyone's head got too large for his or her body, she'd say, 'God opposes the proud but gives grace to the humble.'"

He looked a little chagrined. "When you live with a sports buff, especially a volunteer coach with a winning team, there are plenty of opportunities to use that line."

"She was a smart woman."

"She was that and more." He faded from me a little, like the Cheshire cat wavering in and out before Alice's eyes in Wonderland. Then he returned to the present and asked me a question that startled me.

"What if God *wants* you to be a part of this show?"

"He wouldn't…I can't imagine…surely not…" I stared at him. "Why?"

"I don't know. I've just found that it's wise to check things out with the Big Guy before I discard them summarily, that's all. He works in mysterious ways."

At that moment Ben returned to us burbling over the treasures he'd found in the store, postcards, a polished rock, pencils and other meticulously chosen small items.

"I did good, didn't I, Dad?" He beamed up at his father. "I got a lot of stuff for the money you gave me."

"You certainly did." Jack looked closely at Ben. The child's eyes were unnaturally bright. "You look as though you are about to fall over from exhaustion, buddy. Did you overdo it today?"

"I am kinda tired."

Jack picked up Ben in his arms. "I should have been watching out for you. I let you do too much."

"But it was fun!" Ben leaned forward and grabbed my hand. "It was fun 'cause you came along. Can you come with us next time we go somewhere? Dad says we can go to the Children's Theater sometime soon."

"Let's talk about it later," Jack suggested. "Quinn's probably very tired of us right now."

Tired of them? I'm not sure that would be possible.

Much later, Jack's odd inquiry was still floating through my mind.

What if God did want me to take the *Chrysalis* job?

Jack had said it. God works in mysterious ways.

Could that include a cheesy television show that is going to make mental cases out of some perfectly nice, normal people before the producers get through playing with their minds?

Chapter Fourteen

I dumped milk onto my Rice Krispies and sliced a banana over the top.

Maggie didn't look up from her cereal bowl.

I always know when she's depressed by what she eats for breakfast. When things are going well, she has a finger-wide sliver of cantaloupe, a strawberry she slices paper thin, a hard-boiled egg and a rye crisp.

Today she was eating what she'd brought home from her trip to the grocery store—garishly colored presweetened cereal that was turning the half-and-half she'd poured over it an odd shade of lavender. There were crusts of heavily buttered slices of cinnamon raisin bread littering the table around her dish and an enormous tumbler of chocolate milk poised by her hand for easy access. I'd had to stop her from drinking the chocolate milk straight out of the carton and make her pour it into a glass.

Self-destruction takes many forms. Saturated fats,

synthetic dyes, artificial flavors and preservatives are Maggie's.

"Don't you have a tryout today? Maybe you'd be more on top of your game if…" I picked up the cereal box with little brightly colored gizmos doing the jitterbug on its front. "What is this stuff?"

"I saw it advertised on Saturday when I was watching cartoons. Kids are supposed to love it."

"Cartoons? Oh, Maggie, you have to snap out of this!"

"Give me a little more time, okay?" She held out her hand. "And pass me the cereal, will you?"

I clutched it to my chest. "What time is your appointment?"

Maggie peered at the clock and her eyes widened. "I didn't realize how late it was. I'm going to be late for my manicure."

"I could give you one if you want."

"No thanks. The audition is for a hand model. I can't have a homemade manicure for that."

She disappeared into her room and came out twenty minutes later with her hair twisted tightly on the top of her head. It pulled a little at the corners of her eyes, making her look even more exotic than usual. She wore a neat suit and three-inch heels and looked like she'd been hanging out in a *Vogue* magazine advertisement until only moments ago.

"Fabulous!"

"Whatever. Wish me luck." Maggie disappeared in a waft of perfume.

Luck? I don't think so. Prayer? That's what I'm into.

Dash, who had already been outside for his morning

ablutions inexplicably decided I needed to go for a walk. He approached me, carrying his leash in his mouth, dropped it on the toes of my slippers, ran to the door and whined.

"I can't play with you, Dash. I have to do lesson plans."

He collapsed into a pitiful leggy lump on the floor and gave a whimper that would have moved a heart of stone.

"I'll walk you later."

He gave a high-pitched whine, let his head fall to the floor and covered his long sleek nose with his paws.

"Well, if you're going to be like that…"

He was on his feet in one quick, graceful movement and I had a glimpse of the athlete lurking beneath his couch-potato persona.

I glared at him sternly. "A ten-minute walk, that's it. Unless you can help me figure out a new science unit, I have to get busy."

He shivered with anticipatory glee while I tied my tennis shoes. I hooked his leash to his collar and when I opened the door he burst through it, nearly dragging me into the doorjamb face-first.

Purposefully, he towed me toward the small park across the street and headed for a large flower bed that held mass plantings of bright purple, pink, yellow and white blooms. There were coneflowers, black-eyed susans, cosmos, daylilies, geraniums and several others I couldn't identify, all chosen for one purpose—to attract butterflies.

The butterfly garden is one of Dash's favorite places. He sits on his haunches and stares unflinchingly as butterflies alight on the flowers. I wonder what he thinks as he sits there, mesmerized by the delicate winged creatures as they flutter around their chosen blooms.

Usually I can read Dash's mind. There are several recurrent themes in his repertoire. These involve eating, licking, chewing, sniffing, running, playing and dreaming about wooden rabbits. He's no Einstein but he is consistent.

As we sat in the sun watching the dip and flutter of the butterflies hovering over the garden, a lightbulb flashed on in my brain. I grabbed Dash's snout and gave him a big kiss. "Dash, you are brilliant. Thanks for the idea."

He looked at me as though I were one or two biscuits short of a box but stood up when I pulled on his leash.

Bugs, of course. What better lesson plan for little boys who would soon be completing a study of the solar system? We could study butterflies and the plants that attracted them, beetles (little boys love beetles) and, just for a touch of the gross and yucky that kids enjoy, a centipede and a cockroach or two.

I just love being a teacher.

I was wrapped up in the discovery that centipedes could have anywhere from fifty to two hundred legs and considered not answering the telephone when it rang. As usual, curiosity got the best of me in the end.

It was Ben, his voice high-pitched and excited, talking so fast I could barely understand him.

"Nathan and his mom and dad can't so he gave them to me and my dad can and he told me I could invite a friend and I invite *you*."

"Can and can't what, Ben? I'm not following you."

I heard him sigh with disgust and then "Here, Dad, you tell her. She doesn't get it."

Jack's voice came on the line. He was laughing. "I can't imagine how anyone could 'get' that garbled message. Hello, Quinn, how are you?"

"Just fine." Now, at least, thanks to you.

"Linda just came over with three tickets to the circus. Apparently they are going out of town and won't be able to use them. I told Ben I'd take him and any one of his friends as long as they minded their manners and didn't get too rowdy. And the friend he's picked is you. Please don't feel like we're stalking you, trying to take you every place we go, but Ben's rather—" he lowered his voice "—infatuated with you."

"As I am with him. He's a darling boy, Jack. I'm flattered that he likes me, but don't you think he'd have more fun with another ten-year-old?"

"Please come with us, please, please, please?" I heard in the background at Jack's house.

"Not according to him. You're his first, second and third picks."

"How can a girl resist?"

So Ben sat between us with a box of popcorn, a huge plastic bag of cotton candy, a soda in a quartsized glass and a monkey that bobbled on the end of a stick. On his head was a ringmaster's hat. At a facepainting booth, he'd been made up to look like a whitefaced clown. Now he sat staring intently at the high-wire act.

He turned to his father. "Can I sit down there, Dad?

He pointed to an empty aisle seat four rows down. Just for a minute? I want to get closer."

"Come back up here when this act is over."

"Okay." Ben jammed the hat more tightly onto his head, picked up his popcorn and made his way to the new seat.

"He's limping a little," I observed.

"A flare-up. He's a trouper though." Jack looked grim as he watched his son. "I wish I had his fighting spirit."

"Are you sure you don't?"

"My fighting spirit burned out, Quinn. Sometimes I wonder how I'll keep it up for Ben, yet I have to put a smile on my face and be a positive force that keeps him going."

He gazed blankly at the colorful arena filled with tumbling clowns, people flying through the air and trumpeting elephants. "Losing Emily really took it out of me, and now Ben needs me even more."

Then Jack slapped the palms of his hands on the tops of his thighs and willed a smile onto his face. "We're at the circus. You don't need to listen to this. Let's have fun."

Although Ben managed to do so, Jack and I both sat for the rest of the afternoon under the cloudy sky of our conversation.

"Want to go to a fund-raiser with me?" Pete sounded excited. I held the telephone receiver away from my ear and looked at it in disbelief.

"Why? Aren't you planning on bringing a beautiful girl who will look up at you and bat her eyelashes?"

"Very funny. I'm between girls right now and you know it. Besides, you're beautiful. Just don't bring your batty eyelashes anywhere near me."

"What are we raising funds for?"

"To send disabled kids to summer camp, places where they can play baseball, swim, ride horses, that kind of stuff. I had a cousin who went to a camp for diabetic kids when he was young. He said those were some of the greatest times in his life because at camp he actually felt 'normal.' I wanted to be involved in the community somehow, so I started giving donations to the group. Tonight they are having their big fund-raiser of the year and I bought two tickets."

"If you really mean it, I suppose I can come. Maggie is going for a massage this evening and won't be home until late."

"I'll pick you up at seven. Wear something fabulous. It's black-tie."

No pressure, I thought as I dressed. Pete sets a high standard. "Fabulous" cannot usually be pulled together in fifteen minutes.

"You look great, Quinn," Maggie commented as she left the house at six forty-five in tattered jeans and a bleach-stained sweatshirt.

"So do you, although I can't see why in that outfit. Most people would put it in the garbage. Casual suits you."

"Good. Get used to it. Now that my modeling career is over, all I'll be wearing is frayed jeans and thread-bare rags."

"Glad you don't like to exaggerate."

Maggie smiled faintly, stepped back into the foyer and gave me a hug. "I love you, Quinn. You are the best friend a girl could ever have."

"And the feeling is likewise. But you have to—"

"I know, I know. Snap out of this. Get back to work." A shadow crossed her features. "I just can't figure out how to do it this time. I've been down before, but this is different. My battery is dead, Quinn."

Hers and Jack's both, apparently. "Then you need a jump start, something different and exciting. I'm praying for that for you already."

"Thanks, kiddo, you're the best." She glanced at her watch. "I'd better go. Have fun at the fund-raiser."

When my quasi-date Pete came to the door to pick me up I gave him a once-over. "You are the most darling little penguin I have ever seen. Love the tux."

He kissed me on the cheek. "I knew I was doing the right thing by asking you. Every former girlfriend of mine who is there will be slack jawed with envy when they see you. New dress?"

"This ol' thang?" I spun for him to see the dress I'd been offered after a shoot. The lining had been ripped, one spaghetti strap had been damaged and it was a foot longer than anyone else could wear. I had volunteered to buy it. I grew up in 4-H. I can mend a dress with the best of them. I repaired the lining and replaced the missing strap with a string of pearls and, voilà, had a willowy black-sequined, pencil-thin dress that makes me look nine feet tall.

Until Pete invited me to the gala, I hadn't paid much attention to the trumpeting and fanfare this particular event was garnering. I had noticed it mentioned in the paper several times, however, and when we got to the country club where it was being held, I revised my image of Pete's idea of charity.

"This place is crawling with professional athletes, journalists and some of the Cities' most successful people. Why didn't you tell me?" I spoke through my teeth as I smiled and nodded while navigating a sea of glittery dresses and tuxedos.

"I did. You didn't pay any attention. Did you think I'd ask you to a bake sale? This event brings in a lot of money for disabled and disadvantaged kids. It provides outlets for them through athletics and camping experiences. Cool, huh?"

Very cool. And it got cooler or maybe warmer, like my cheeks, when I saw Jack Harmon making his way toward us from across the room.

Pete's gaze followed mine. "Who are you looking at…oh, hello, there. Good-looking guy, Quinn. Is he who I think he is?"

"He's the father of one of my new students. Don't jump to conclusions. You'll hurt yourself."

The pristine white of Jack's shirt made his tanned skin even darker and the brown of his eyes more penetrating. Pete jabbed me in the ribs as if to say, *Why didn't you tell me you knew this guy?*

Not that I would—or should—have. Jack and I were conducting business, not pleasure.

"I had no idea you'd be here tonight, Quinn. I'm delighted to see you." Jack moved comfortably in the crowd as if he'd done it a million times before. The reserve I'd observed earlier seemed to have been banished for the night.

"Do you come to many of these?" I asked politely.

Pete gave a strangled cough. I turned to pound him on the back. His face was red with embarrassment.

"Quinn, this is *the* Jack Harmon! He used to play hockey with the U of M—a star forward. He's been doing fund-raisers ever since. He's done more good for kids' sports in the last ten years than anyone else I know—programs for low-income families, kids with disabilities…" Pete pumped Jack's hand with delight, obviously a fan.

"Quinn, Jack is the organizer of this evening. If you get this guy to back your charity you can count on a success."

Jack reddened. "You give me too much credit."

My stomach did flips and my heart thudded wildly. The man had many facets not revealed by building a volcano or scouring a museum.

"I'd like to stay and visit longer," Jack said apologetically, "but there are a lot of people here that I need to greet. Perhaps we could get together again later? After dinner when things are winding up?"

"Sure, no problem." Pete pumped Jack's hand again. "Great to meet you. I had no idea my friend Quinn knew people in such high places."

As he said it, he took a step to the right to dodge the elbow he knew I'd send his way. That almost made me tumble sideways and Jack reached out to steady me. His eyes glinted with amusement. "Later?"

"Sure." *Later.*

After Jack was gone, Pete turned to me. "You mean

you didn't know? Jack Harmon is a very influential man in this community. I can't believe you haven't heard of him!"

"My friend Linda said he was athletic and had done some fund-raising. How was I to know?"

"I'm glad I got to meet him." Pete still looked a little awestruck. "You said his son is ill and can't play competitive sports. That must be tough for a guy like Jack. I'm sure he'd want to hand the torch on to his son."

I hadn't thought of that. My admiration for him grew.

Pete made an odd, strangling sound in his throat. "You've got to be kidding me. What are they doing here?"

Making their way through the crowd, I saw Eddie Bessett and a lovely young woman with light brown hair and green eyes. She was laughing and Eddie smiled down at her with benevolent affection.

"I suppose Eddie read about it in the paper and decided to contribute. It's a good cause. I can't believe I knew so little about it." I stared at the woman on Eddie's arm. "Is that his date? She's lovely."

The delicate beauty wore a gauzy taupe dress that, on anyone else, might have looked like rags. She wore it cinched high on her waist. The belt alone had no doubt cost hundreds of dollars. Her jewelry was stark, simple and elegant. She wore drop earrings made of brown gemstones and a ruby ring on her left hand. In a room full of expensive, stylish dresses, hers still stood out.

Pete made that sound again and he was pale as a sheet. "Are you okay, Pete? You look as though you've seen a ghost."

To my surprise he nodded in the affirmative. "I have.

Eddie's sister Kristy. The one I used to date. That's who is with Eddie."

I studied the girl carefully. So this was Pete's love, the one he shouldn't have left behind.

"There you are!" Eddie roared to Pete. "I've been hauling Kristy all over this joint looking for you. I wanted her to see once and for all that she didn't miss a thing by not marrying you." He turned to his sister and spoke cheerfully, as if Pete weren't even there. "See? Nothing but the little twerp I always said he was."

"Eddie!" Her voice was soft and musical, just as I had expected it to be. And the smile she turned on Pete could have melted steel. "Hi, Pete. Long time no see."

Pete was having a hard time keeping his knees from buckling. I didn't blame him. This lovely apparition appearing before *my* eyes was surprising enough. What must he be feeling?

"Kristy. You're more beautiful than ever. I didn't think it was possible." Pete's voice grew soft and intimate.

"Don't pay any attention to him. He's ancient history," Eddie advised jovially. "Besides, he can't even talk our first choice for hostess of *Chrysalis* into taking the job." He turned to me. "Hello, Quinn. I'd like you to meet my sister."

As we exchanged pleasantries, I marveled at Pete's obscenely bad decision to not marry this girl. She is exquisite, funny and sweet and not in all the years I've known Pete have I ever seen him so moonstruck. I'm glad that he brought me and not someone he's been dating to this gala. His poor date wouldn't have had a chance.

A gentle gong rang out, signaling that the silent auction was wrapping up in another room and the mixer had come to an end.

I was surprised to see Jack Harmon hurrying toward me as we searched for our seats the vast room set with white linen, mirrored tiles and glittering candles.

"Quinn, I just got a call from a couple who is supposed to sit at my table. They have a sick child at home and are taking him to the emergency room. I thought perhaps you and Pete would like to join me up front." His eyes twinkled. "It's an unobstructed view of the stage."

"We also have an extra seat," Eddie volunteered. "Frank was supposed to come with us but he got tied up at the last minute. The seat next to Kristy is empty, as well. Too bad. I could have bought a condo in Maui for the price of these tickets."

My brain kicked into high gear just as it had during a school trip in senior high when Pete had had a crush on the head cheerleader. No one had taken the seat next to hers on the school bus so I took matters into my own hands. Just as I'd shoved Pete into the seat next to Betsy Carmichael back than, I figuratively thrust him into the chair by Kristy now.

"Pete, why don't you sit with Eddie and his sister and I'll sit with Jack. I know the two of you have lots to catch up on."

He stared at me as if he'd had a lobotomy.

I shoved him a little and he swayed. "Pete?"

He looked at Eddie's sister and I saw a gooey, syrupy longing in his eyes that he usually saves for melted-in-the-middle chocolate cake or photos of baby greyhounds. "Don't you want to?"

"I…ah…sure. Why not? If you don't mind, Quinn. I don't want to leave you…."

Of course he did. A choice between me and Eddie's sister? No contest. Jack grabbed my arm. "Perfect. But I have to get up front. Come on, Quinn. We can meet these folks after the program for coffee." And he towed me away much like Ben had tugged me around the museum.

Grinning to myself, I followed him, feeling rather smug that I'd helped Cupid deliver an arrow in Pete and Kristy's direction.

Chapter Fifteen

~⚬~

What had I done? I wondered as Jack seated me at a table only steps from the stage and podium. Granted, I'd given Pete a hearty shove in the right direction—I know infatuation when I see it—but I'd also negotiated myself into a primo seat next to Mr. Jack Harmon, fund-raiser extraordinaire. I could tell, by the curious stares, that people were wondering who it was filling the chair next to Jack. He had no doubt been flying solo in the companion department since the death of his wife.

Terrific. By trying to help Pete I may have accidentally navigated myself into tomorrow's gossip columns.

See if I ever do anything nice for you again, Pete Moore!

A tall but spindly topiary centerpiece was too small to hide behind. Fortunately, I do know how to paste a smile on my face and pose for the public. These were the talents I put into use tonight, for what might be the longest continuous photo shoot of my life.

Then again, I didn't give my dinner partner nearly

enough credit for being charming and distracting me from this awkwardness.

"Do you want this?" He shoved a plate with two tiny toast points dotted with caviar.

"I have some, thanks."

"You don't like fish eggs on cardboard, either, huh?"

"It's very elegant. Pete said we paid a thousand dollars a seat for this event. We'd better eat the food."

Jack's white teeth flashed in a grinned. "Amazing, isn't it? This is our biggest event yet. We're going to fund a lot of programs with this money." He lowered his voice conspiratorially. "Frankly, I'm usually too busy to eat at these things. Normally I stop at a fast-food restaurant on the way home after the party and grab a couple burgers and a shake."

Sounds good to me.

"I had no idea you were such a public figure. I didn't imagine you in any role except that of Ben's father."

"That's my best and most important position. Any other falls a far second." He shuffled some cards he'd pulled out of his breast pocket. "I'd better review my notes since I'm the master of ceremonies."

So much for convincing myself that no one would look this way. While Pete was at a back table renewing a relationship with an old flame, the only thing flaming at this table were my cheeks.

It wasn't all bad, though. I got to study Jack up close and watch the play of his facial expressions. He loved this, it was obvious, and his pure delight at visiting with people who stopped by the table was catching.

"I'd like you to meet my son's tutor, Quinn Hunter,"

he said a number of times, introducing me with such pride and satisfaction that my cheeks grew rosy with pleasure. One of Jack's skills is to make anyone feel like a VIP. Occasionally he would absently rest his hand on my shoulder.

That, in itself, wasn't unusual. The congestion around the tables made him graze my arm more than once. What was curious was my response to his touch. A pleasant shiver zippered through me each time our bodies brushed.

It was almost a relief, when, after dinner, Jack rose and moved to the stage. The ballroom darkened and large screens dropped silently from the ceiling. A video began to play as Jack spoke.

"I want you to see what your contributions have done in the past year. Because of your generosity, hundreds of disabled children have had experiences that normal children take for granted."

The next fifteen minutes were a revelation to me and to many in the room. There were photos of start-up facilities for athletic camps for disabled children. They were directed at those with diabetes, emotional, learning or behavioral disabilities, speech and hearing impairments...and the list went on. In addition, many camping weeks, counselors, physicians and therapists were added to already existing camps so that more children could be accommodated. Photos of laughing children filled the screen.

"I have to admit that this year I have an ulterior motive for this fund-raiser," Jack said. "It's purely self-serving on my part, but I believe that ultimately it will be a gift and a blessing to untold numbers of children and their families.

"Funds for Kids has considered sponsoring several weeks of camp to a group we haven't served before. I have personally campaigned long and hard for our committee to open a camp for children with juvenile arthritis." He paused, gathering his thoughts.

"As some of you may know, I have a ten-year-old son who suffers from JA. I've watched firsthand how much he's suffered and how brave he is. Ben is my hero. I aspire to be as courageous, as cheerful and as uncomplaining as he and I'm not sure I'll ever make it."

The large room grew more silent still, the crowd holding its collective breath, waiting to hear what Jack would say next.

"The things I've found Ben resists doing most— exercising his joints, taking medication, resting—are the things he doesn't see his friends doing. There are times he simply can't keep up with them or he has to sit on the sidelines and watch them play a game. He desperately wants to feel normal." Jack looked into the crowd and it was as if he were trying to make eye contact with each and every person. "Don't we all?"

A rustle of recognition spread through the room.

"That's why I feel so passionately about sending Ben to a JA camp. It is one place he gets to fit in. One place he *is* normal. Everyone there has medication to take and exercises to do. Kids wear out and need to rest. No one is left on the sidelines." Emotion crackled in his voice.

"I want my child to feel typical, acceptable, ordinary.

I don't ask that he be happy twenty-four hours a day, but I do ask that there be a place for him to go where 'keeping up' isn't a full-time job. I want him to play with his peers, to laugh, to act like a kid and not feel that he's different from everyone else."

Jack's eyes blazed with passion and I felt swept into his vision. "I've talked to the kids who go to our camps. Many of them say it is the best time of their lives. Now, for purely selfish reasons, I want that for my son—and for all the children just like him."

I felt tears scratching at my eyes.

"One day at school, Ben was too stiff to sit down on the floor cross-legged for his reading circle. When his teacher brought him a chair to sit on, some of his classmates started to laugh at him. Can you imagine how that felt? And can you imagine being in a place where *everyone* understands, where *they* can laugh at the situation and exchange ideas about how to handle an incident like this?"

A little ripple spread through the room as people shifted uncomfortably, trying to imagine it for themselves.

"That's why our work, *your* work, is so important. Give a child a week or two of relief from the stress of having to keep up with his peers.

"I want a place for my son to go for a week each summer that is adapted to his needs. A place he can have a safe, educational and recreational experience that provides him with normalcy and fun. I would like him to meet with other children who understand what it is like to live with pain and to see how they cope. I want him to escape for just a little while, to be a kid and to feel normal and free.

"As a parent of a child with juvenile arthritis, I can't tell you how important it is for these children to feel a sense of accomplishment, to build their self-worth and self-esteem. Ben needs to be treated like any other kid. It's hard, sometimes, to teach him self-discipline and persistence when he is not feeling well, yet it is even more important for him. He has to live for the rest of his life with his physical issues. I want to give him every tool and every opportunity to become the man he's destined to be."

There wasn't a dry eye in the place, I realized. Mine certainly weren't.

"The committee has graciously agreed with me. This year our fund-raiser is dedicated to earning monies to provide camping experiences for children with juvenile arthritis. You know that all our camps in the past have been successful and you have my *personal promise* that this one will meet and exceed our already high standards."

As I watched him, I couldn't help but feel delight and admiration for this man I'd just come to know. Although Ben had had a series of hard knocks, he had one big blessing—his father.

"Our closing activity tonight will be an auction. All funds will go directly into the JA fund, and your generosity will determine how many weeks of JA camp we will sponsor, the quality of the staff and the scope of activities we offer."

Jack gestured toward the man sitting directly across from me. "We have an auctioneer here to take your bids on a new hybrid car generously donated by one of our sponsors."

He was drowned out by clapping, which continued for several minutes, as Jack relinquished the microphone while someone drove a bright green hybrid car onto the stage.

When Jack slipped off the stage to sit beside me again, I could see beads of sweat on his forehead. That speech had not been easy for him.

He leaned closer and I smelled the fresh scent of his aftershave. "I hope somebody bids on it. I'd hate for this car to go for less than sticker price."

"Surely that won't happen, not after what you said about the new camp."

"I want this so desperately for Ben. Maybe I sounded selfish promoting this particular camp, but if people knew kids like Ben and the upward climb they have…"

He didn't have to worry.

One by one, bidders waved their placards in the air and the bid rocketed. Twenty thousand, thirty, then forty. By the time the car sold, someone had donated nearly sixty-five thousand dollars to the cause, double what the car was worth.

My head was spinning as I mentally tallied the money this evening had raised. The success was obvious by the number of people who wanted to talk to Jack and to congratulate him.

It took forty five minutes for us to work our way from the front of the room to the back as Jack was inundated with well-wishers. People stuffed checks made out to the cause into his pockets. Much to my delight, people quit staring at me to focus completely on Jack.

We met Eddie, Pete and Kristy outside the banquet-room doors.

"That went well," Eddie said drily. "You collected more than four hundred thousand dollars tonight."

"For a good cause," Pete chimed in.

"For a *great* cause." Eddie whipped a check out of his breast pocket. "Here's my meager contribution."

Eddie had his thumb over part of the dollar amount for which the check was written, but I did see at least three zeros in front of the decimal point. Not bad. Not bad at all.

Jack's emotions lay on the surface for all to see as he took the check. His vulnerability and sincerity had inspired generosity as much as anything else on the program tonight.

"I promised you coffee."

"Listen, about that…" Pete shifted restlessly from one foot to the other. "I know this sounds really rude, but Kristy wants to get back to the hotel and Eddie ran into some fellows he'd like to visit with. I told Kristy I could run her home, but that would leave Quinn without a ride."

"It's fine, Pete. You don't have to do that," Kristy protested, but Pete shushed her. The rat had no intention of driving me home when he could have her.

Jack, whose attention had been drawn away by someone walking past, turned his head and spoke over his shoulder. "No problem, I'll drop her off."

Pete winked at me. "Great. We'll see you later then. Thanks for a fabulous evening." Then he and his friends melted into the crowd as if they'd never even existed, leaving me dependent on Jack to find my way home.

Touché. I'd dumped Pete in the lap of a former ladylove and now he was returning the favor. He'd shot Cupid's arrow right back at me—whether I wanted it or not.

We sat in front of the fireplace at a little coffee shop not far from my home. I kicked off my shoes and propped my feet on the hearth while Jack loosened his tie. His jacket was draped over the back of the wing chair in which he sat.

"Where's Ben tonight?"

"Having an overnight with Nathan. He was one excited little boy."

"I had no idea," I admitted ruefully. "that I was roaming the Science Museum with a celebrity."

"Quasi-celebrity," he corrected. "By the way, what's the deal with your friend Pete and that woman you sent him off with tonight? I detected a little matchmaking going on."

"A former girlfriend. I didn't even know about her until I met her brother. They are in town because he is the producer of *Chrysalis* and they are filming here. Pete kept his mouth shut about her all these years, which tells me that something pretty serious went on between them.

"Pete tells Maggie and me everything. Not mentioning this woman probably means he'd considered marrying her."

"You know him best," Jack commented, looking amused. "Mind reading has never been one of my strong suits."

"Perhaps you haven't known anyone as long or as well as I have known Pete. We grew up in houses on the same street, shared a dentist, a pediatrician and a trampoline. He broke his arm and I cried. Except for the few years he lived in California, we were never apart. Pete's a brother to me."

"So you never thought about him romantically?"

"Eww. Best way ever to ruin a good friendship."

"That's true. When it gets romantic you either end up estranged or married, don't you? How about you? Any loves in your life?"

"I'm between relationships right now. Perhaps I'm waiting for love at first sight. It's nice to know it really exists."

Jack picked up my hand as it lay on the arm of my wing chair. "Don't marry just anyone. You are very special woman, Quinn. Wait for the perfect one. I did and I've never regretted it. Emily is all I ever wanted and needed—or ever will."

Ever? That makes it clear. Jack has been to the mountaintop and that is that. Too bad. He's the kind of man *I* could love, but I'd never want a man who couldn't love me back.

"I know a great little place that makes the best malts in three states. It's not just everyone who knows how much malt powder to use. And their fries are out of this world. Oh, yes, and there's this half-pound burger with guacamole and olives."

"I'd love to."

He looked so delighted that I nearly laughed out loud. Jack doesn't know me well enough, yet. I'd have no trouble outeating him and enjoying every minute of it. Granted, I'm not a cheap date—appetizers, entrees and dessert—but I'm wonderful company.

"Let's go then. It's only fifteen minutes from here."

The place looked like a dive, but what it lacked in ambience it made up for in flavor.

Over a haystack of French fries, Jack smiled at me. "Thank you for joining me this evening. You made it much more pleasurable for me. Sometimes after an event like this I'm restless and going straight home seems anticlimactic. This is nice."

It's sad to think that a vibrant man like this one had so isolated himself. Still, if he was determined never to allow another woman into his life, what choice did he have?

I pushed away the melancholy thought and reached for the dessert menu. Jack, watching me, burst out laughing.

Chapter Sixteen

Maggie, Pete and I sat in the vast open space of Pete's loft above his studio. Sunshine streamed through the floor-to-ceiling windows. I, much to Pete's annoyance, wore sunglasses.

"You're inside my house, Quinn. You take off your hat and mittens when you come in the winter. Now it's time to take off your sunglasses."

"Pull the drapes then. I'll go blind in here." Pete's place is decorated with glossy wood floors, glimmering stainless steel and shining reflective pieces made of bits of mirror.

"You are supposed to enjoy sunshine. It's a glorious day."

"How can I if I can't open my eyes long enough to see it?"

We bickered contentedly just as we always have. Today our familiar pattern was particularly comforting. Pete and I are not victims of the "familiarity breeds contempt" school of thought. In our case, familiarity just breeds more familiarity. Not that it's always a good thing, mind you, but it explains a lot about the way Pete, Maggie and I interact.

"Why didn't you ever mention Kristy Bessett before recently, Pete? I thought we agreed to tell each other everything." Maggie's tone was accusing.

"Ha. There's no way I'd agree to that. I don't want to know everything about you. That's way too much information."

"He was out in California then. Maybe she was just one of many—"

"She was not!" Then his face turned red as he realized he'd been caught. "Quinn, you tricked me."

"Like catching trout in a bathtub, Pete. You're too easy."

Resigned, he began his story. "Kristy and I met at a gathering of some mutual friends, that's all. We had fun together. She's a very nice girl."

"Come off it, Pete. What happened? Why'd you break up?"

He sat quietly, twirling his cup, splashing coffee up and out over the rim. "Because I'm a fool, an idiot, an imbecile and a clod."

"Oh, just *that*. You've always been that." Maggie yawned and stretched, catlike, on the couch.

He glared at her. "Because I had this idea that I was going to make it to the big time and I didn't want to have a wife and kids holding me back."

That bit of information hovered in our midst like a thundercloud.

"So I dumped her."

"You are right. You were an imbecile. She's wonderful." I stroked Flash's warm fur as he lay immobilized in the sunlight.

"I talked myself into thinking that I'd put her on a pedestal and that she wasn't nearly so desirable as I imagined."

"But after seeing her again you've realized that she actually was all you'd believed?"

"And more. I really blew it, didn't I?"

"Eddie said she isn't married."

"It doesn't make any difference. She doesn't want anything to do with me. I didn't realize at first how much I'd hurt her. She's scared of me now. She no longer trusts me not to disappoint her."

"Can you blame her?"

"Not a bit. The responsibility for being a louse falls on me."

He held out a plate of foil-wrapped dark espresso chocolates, an obvious ploy to change the subject. "Candy?"

It looked a little squishy to me. "May I put it the refrigerator first so it doesn't get all over my hands?"

"It's not that hot in here, it's…" His voice trailed away as Maggie stood up and headed for the coffee table.

"I'll take chocolate." She picked up the dish and strolled back to her chair at the kitchen table. "I don't care if it is messy."

She opened a piece and began to lick the liquefied chocolate off the foil wrapper.

Maggie hadn't done anything but eat since we'd arrived. First the grilled salmon and mixed-green salad

Pete had provided, three buns from Wuollet's bakery slathered with butter, two dishes of Rocky Road ice cream smothered in caramel and chocolate sauces, a Godiva truffle she found on Pete's counter and now this.

Randy's leaving may have triggered her downward spiral, but losing the health-club job was corkscrewing her further into her depths. If there is an abyss, Maggie is poised on its rim.

We know the signs, of course. Whenever I get down in the dumps, I turn to exercise. I jog on the treadmill until sweat is flying off me like water off a wet dog. Then I stand in the hottest shower I can tolerate and mutter to myself. After that I go to bed with a Bible and a cozy pillow and sleep it off.

Pete retreats into music, usually soaring church hymns from the late 1700s or 1800s or, paradoxically, show tunes. He downloads the score from *Oklahoma!* or *South Pacific* into his iPod and moves his hands in time with the music until his frustration passes.

Maggie tries to drown her sorrows in food.

Finally I walked to the table and took the candy dish away. She stared at the spot where it had been. "What did you do that for?"

"Because you always tell me to stop you when you get down. Because no matter how much you think you want to do something, you always regret it later. You hired me to be the gatekeeper that keeps junk out of your mouth."

"We were in eighth grade and I thought I had a pouch for a belly. The diet was supposed to last a week, not fifteen years. You can quit anytime now."

"Can't. It's ingrained in my bones. Besides, you don't even taste that stuff you're jamming down your throat."

"I might as well eat myself into a stupor," Maggie moaned. "First Randy, then the health-club disaster. What's the point of trying anymore?"

She rested her chin in her hands and studied herself in one of Pete's many pieces of mirrored art, a large vase filled with sunflowers that sat in the center of the table.

"If only I could…"

The silence that followed was tense. Maggie's "if onlys" had caused us trouble more than once.

"I want you to tell me more about that job offer you got, Quinn. The one for that reality-television show."

"Not much to tell. I haven't pursued it."

"But you've got a chance at being the host of the show?" Maggie skewered me with a look. "Take it! You'd be awesome.

"I don't understand why, when you have a big chance, you consider turning it down. It's a job, after all." She plucked at the elasticized waistband of her workout pants. "Maybe the club was right to decide against me as their model. They realized something I didn't—that I was going to double in size in the next couple months."

"If you keep licking melted chocolate off candy wrappers, you might, but otherwise there's no danger."

"At least with hand modeling I don't have to worry so much. I have very slender fingers." Maggie waggled her piano octave-straddling digits. Not a hangnail in sight.

"Speaking of that—" her brow furrowed "—I thought I would have heard by now…."

Her cell phone rang. "I'll bet this is the call." She dug

her phone out of her pocket and flipped it open and said brightly, "Maggie here."

"So she does know how to be cheerful." Pete moved closer to me. "She should try it on us sometime."

"Maggie is venting. She doesn't have to put on a mask for us."

I flinched as Maggie's cell phone unexpectedly flew through the air and hit the wall behind me.

"Whoa," Pete muttered as we both spun to stare at her. "What's up?"

Maggie jumped to her feet and began to pace the floor, flapping her arms and raging at no one in particular. "I can't believe it! It's totally ridiculous. Mine are perfectly fine. Great. People tell me so."

"Maggie?" Pete ventured.

She looked up, her eyes wide and furious. "Those… those…idiots!"

"Which idiots are you referring to specifically? There are plenty of them out there."

"The hand-lotion idiots. This is ageism or just plain idiot-ism. I can't believe it!"

Idiotism?

"They turned me down for the hand-modeling job. Said my hands looked more 'mature' than they wanted for the product because the market is for teens and college-aged women. I know exactly who they hired. The girl after me was fourteen years old and had spiders painted onto her fake nails!"

"Spiders?" Pete echoed. "Why would anyone paint spiders on their nails?"

Maggie was still ranting. "If they'd had to choose

from photos of hands, they would have picked mine. But because they saw how much older I was than the *child* after me—"

"You don't know that, Maggie."

Her shoulders sagged as the truth of my words hit home. She collapsed heavily into Pete's chair, too depleted to rant anymore. "I can't even get a job as a hand model. First Randy, then the health club and now this. What am I going to do?"

"This is just temporary, Mag," Pete attempted to reassure her.

"We all go through rough spots in this business."

Pete and I offered all the platitudes and tired expressions that don't help one iota. Who really does know what to say when the rug of a friend's life is pulled out from under her? Although we attempted to minimize the damage done by her latest disappointment, talking to Maggie is like convincing a brick wall that it is actually a basket of flowers. Not easy.

When Maggie disappeared into the bathroom, I voiced my frustration aloud. "Why is self-esteem so hard to come by?"

Pete chewed nervously on his lower lip. "Probably because we have the idea that we can earn it by ourselves."

I curled up on his ultracontemporary faux suede couch, which is surprisingly comfortable if you don't mind sitting six inches off the floor. "Tell me it isn't so!" I mocked. "You mean the television commercials that say you'll have more self-esteem if you lose weight, work out, go to school, whiten your teeth and buy a new car are wrong?"

"We're so caught up in the idea that if we buy the right brand of jeans or designer purse it will make us better and more accepted that we don't untangle it to see what's really true."

Pete sank down beside me. His long legs looked even more ridiculous than mine, with his knees splayed near his ears. Then he stretched them out and looked more proportional again. "If we depend on our looks, accomplishments or the praises of others to feel good, we're in big trouble. You and I know that but Maggie…"

"'As I looked at everything I had worked so hard to accomplish, it was all so meaningless. It was like chasing the wind. There was nothing really worthwhile anywhere.'" I quoted. "Even King Solomon struggled with it."

"And the struggle is pointless, like Flash chasing his tail."

Flash, hearing his name, opened one eye and closed it again. Dash, comatose, never twitched.

"My grandmother says that if you are right with God, everything else falls into place." Pete shifted on the couch, looking for a more comfortable position.

I recalled how difficult it had been as a child for me to believe that God wanted to—and could—manage my life for me.

"Thy will be done" were hard words to get out of my mouth. *What about* my *will?* I'd pray. *Maybe You won't give me what I want. Do You even know about that doll I like at Toys 'R' Us?*

It wasn't until I was sixteen, a foot taller than any boy in my class, acne dotted and skinny as a straw that I ran across a bit of scripture that changed my outlook. There was nothing, it seemed, that I could do to make myself shorter or more like the giggly, flirty girls in class who got all the dates.

Trust in the Lord with all your heart, do not depend on your own understanding. Seek His will in all you do…don't be impressed with your own wisdom. Instead, fear the Lord…then you will gain renewed health and vitality.

Corny as it might sound, the verse hit me right between the eyes. I couldn't keep my skin from breaking out or guys calling me "Giraffe" because my legs were so long. I was *glad* there was someplace else to go, something beyond myself to depend upon. I certainly wasn't doing anything special for myself.

When I turned things over to God, my skin didn't miraculously clear up and none of the cute boys immediately grew to match my height, of course, but it somehow didn't matter so much anymore.

That's what Maggie needs right now, to do exactly what that old cliché says, let go and let God.

Instead, she was in the bathroom slathering on hand lotion and thinking of new ways to wear her hair that would make her look less "mature."

"Do you think she'll stay in my bathroom forever?" Pete asked gloomily.

"Not forever. She's got to gather her wits about her though. You remember what it was like for Maggie at home with her sisters. Now, every time she's rejected she's fourteen again and feels unattractive and unwanted."

"She needs to start moving ahead with her life." Pete fiddled with his pencil, tapping the end on his coffee table. "Another bad thing just can't happen."

The scream from the bathroom could have cracked all the mirrors in Pete's house. Both Dash and Flash whined and tried to cover their ears as they lay tangled on Flash's huge red dog bed.

Pete blanched and I felt blood drain from my face, as well. He was the first to his feet and knocked over a chair in his haste to get to the bathroom. I raced after him while Flash and Dash ran in the other direction. They are not conflict-loving animals.

The door was locked. Pete pounded on it so hard I was afraid it might splinter.

"What's wrong in there? Should we call an ambulance? Maggie?"

Finally we heard the lock click open and the door swung away to reveal Maggie still intact with no blood pouring down her head or great gashes on her body.

"What happened?" I demanded.

She lifted her hand, her thumb and forefinger pinched together so tightly that the pads of her fingers were turning white. A single strand of hair was pressed between them. Maggie stared at it as if it had floated down from a flying saucer.

"I found a gray hair."

To most people this is an unpleasant little shock the first time it happens. To Maggie, it was the equivalent of a body blow.

Pete, of course, didn't get it.

"So? You've got black hair and you've always said your family turned gray early. What's the problem?"

Maggie slammed the door in his face.

Men can be so linear and obtuse.

"It's one more knife through the heart. A small one, granted, but it could be the straw, er, hair, that breaks the camel's back."

"We should never have let her go into the bathroom," Pete groaned. "You know how bright the lights in there are."

"Like sitting in a police station getting the third degree."

"It's no wonder she found a gray hair. I'm surprised she didn't find dozens of them. Still, it's nothing a little touch-up won't cure."

My own mother, whose hair is brown, was actually happy when she started to get gray. "Frosted hair without the bill at the salon," she'd say. And it looks good on her, making her striking in a way that Dad says "drives him wild."

To that, Mother mumbles that the only way to tame my wild father is with a dart gun which usually starts a conversation about going on safari and they're off and running. I think Mother enjoys these adventures as much as Dad, although she won't admit it. It was her idea, after all, to dogsled in Alaska to get a feel for what the Iditarod is like.

But for Maggie to find gray hair after being dumped by Randy and losing those jobs is an entirely different matter. She is slipping off the deep end of the pool and Pete and I can't keep rescuing her forever.

"What are we going to do with her, Pete?"

"Pray for her."

I threw my arms around Pete and hugged him until he yelped. Then I gave him a big wet kiss on the cheek. "I love you, Pete, you are so sweet."

"Sweet Pete, Saccharine Pete, that's me." He wiggled out of my grasp. "Now get your hands off me, it's like being kissed my sister. Disgusting."

If I know Maggie as well as I think I do, she's already imagining herself hawking prune juice, denture cream and Depend.

She's probably decided she is the perfect new poster girl for AARP. Not bad for someone not quite thirty yet.

Chapter Seventeen

Settled on our large couch with a bowl of popcorn, a liter of soda and the television remote, we'd been involved in an old-movie marathon for the past two evenings. Maggie is having a difficult time being alone with her own thoughts. My days are taken up with work. I've done several photo shoots in recent days, but I've saved the nights for Maggie.

"Quinn?" Maggie's voice was small and tentative, as if she were building up courage to ask me for a favor.

"Hmm?" I handed her the popcorn, assuming that was what she wanted. We never argue over the remote, but we both like to be the one in possession of the popcorn bowl.

"I have something I want to ask you."

"Okay. Shoot." Engrossed as I was in the previews for an upcoming movie, I didn't give her my full attention. Not, that is, until she said, "I searched Google for *Chrysalis* today."

A little trickle of apprehension bled down my spine. "Oh?"

"It sounds interesting." She said it a little too casually.

"You think so?" I feigned indifference, but my heart pounded harder in my chest. This is exactly what I'd hoped wouldn't happen. She wasn't what Eddie and Frank wanted as hostess of the show and I didn't want her disappointed by another rejection.

"So you really aren't going to take the job as hostess?"

Here it comes. Maggie's going to ask if she can apply for the job.

"Why do you think it's so bad? What's wrong with women having their dreams come true? If they want to look better and they get the chance, I don't see what's wrong with that."

"It's not necessarily bad. People do have things they'd like to change—a scar from an accident, crowded teeth or protruding ears. Maybe they are unhappy with loose skin left over after they lose weight or the chin they inherited from Uncle Ole. But that doesn't mean they go out and ask to be made over from head to toe.

"Shows like this feed people's insecurities and make them think they aren't okay when they truly are."

"But what if they aren't—okay, I mean?"

"In whose estimation? The people who love them? Their friends? God? Seems to me it is important to be right *inside* ourselves first so we have the wisdom and discernment to make decisions about our outsides."

"It's easy for you to say, Quinn. You're beautiful."

"And you're not?" I couldn't keep the incredulity out of my voice.

"This is the twenty-first century, Quinn. It's tough to keep up. Besides, I'm almost thirty. That's old for a model. I don't see anything wrong with having minor nips and tucks if it would help me keep up in my field."

"Times are changing, Mags. There are incredible older models working all the time now. Besides that, neither of us has ever said this is the only career we'd ever have. That would be like trying to keep up with Olympians year after year. They'd keep getting younger and younger while we'd grow older and more decrepit."

"Decrepit, that's me. Thanks for the cheery words, Quinn." She grabbed a pillow and hugged it to her chest. "I don't want to grow old. It's too hard."

"Give me a break, Mag."

I thought she was going to respond, but she seemed to reconsider. "Turn up the sound on the television, will you? And quit hogging that soda."

I was surprised and relieved that she didn't pursue the issue further.

I was looking forward to a reprieve the next afternoon when I rang the Harmons' doorbell. One more encounter with a high-maintenance person this week could bring me to my knees.

Jack opened the door and blinked like a sleepy grizzly bear when the light hit his eyes.

"Sorry. Did I wake you?"

"No. Just watching movies. Come in." He moved aside and I entered the dusky house. The blinds were closed and the curtains pulled. It looked like a movie theater—or a dungeon.

"Dad, is Quinn here?" Ben's small voice came from the family room.

"Come in." Jack led me to the large-screen television flickering in the dimness.

Ben greeted me from the depths of a leather couch. "We're watching old movies. Stuff Dad says he watched when he was a little kid."

"Ben's not feeling well. He couldn't sleep last night and his pain is bad today. I'm thankful that we arranged for you to come. It's difficult for him to be in school like this."

I saw it immediately in Ben's eyes and in the paleness of his skin.

"Are you going to teach me something today?" Ben sounded tired and his little-boy's voice was reedy. "My dad said he'd get my books and lessons from my teacher."

"Are you up to learning something?"

Ben seemed to perk up a little. "What?"

"We could do a science experiment. An ooky one, if you like. We could make slime."

"I don't think...." Jack began to protest but was drowned out by Ben's enthusiastic "Yes!"

"If you have Borax and white glue we're in business."

"In the laundry room. The cleaning lady keeps it pretty well stocked."

Making slime with a man you care about is one of those special moments that just don't happen very often. I'm sure most women are grateful for that.

We measured Borax and water into a solution, mixed it with glue, divided it into zippered plastic bags and hunted through the cupboard looking for food coloring. All the time we discussed how the Borax

was responsible for connecting the glue molecules together to make the thick, slimy gel with which Ben
was entranced.

"You can't feed this to the dog or to other little kids,"
I warned. "And please don't put it in the carpet."

Ben let the stuff ooze through his fingers and smiled.
"I like this." He played with the slime for several minutes
before his smile began to falter. "Dad, I'm tired."

"I'll go," I offered, hoping I hadn't exacerbated his
weariness.

"Wait. I'll tuck you in on the couch, Ben. You can rest
while Quinn and I visit in the other room." Jack lifted
his son so gently than Ben could have been made of soap
bubbles and he would not have broken.

I finished cleaning up our project and then went to
the formal living room at the front of the house. Jack
had pulled the drapery open a crack and was staring out
into the street.

"He likes it dark when he's tired and hurting," Jack said
absently. His chiseled features grew melancholy. "It com-
forts him. He's been that way ever since he was little."

Much to my unease I realized I wished I could draw
my finger along his jawline and put my arms around him
to comfort him. Instead I said, "Ben is *still* little."

"I know." Jack's shoulders sagged. "I wish it were
me, Quinn. I'd be happy to trade places with Ben so that
he could have a chance at being a normal child."

His gaze pierced through me. "I wanted to trade
places with Emily, too, but that couldn't happen, either."
Then Jack's even teeth flashed in a faint, lopsided grin.
"It's a good thing you came by. I was feeling pretty sorry

for myself. Every time Ben goes through a good stretch I convince myself that we've got it licked. Then…"

"I've been reading about juvenile arthritis. It sounds as if treatment has improved."

"Dramatically." He gestured for me to sit down on one end of the couch while he took the other. "I should be grateful that they can prevent JA from being as crippling as it once was. My wife's uncle suffered from the same disease and his joints became so gnarled that it hurt to look at him. He didn't complain though. Maybe that's where Ben gets his bravery."

"When Ben isn't doing well, you really wish his mother was here, don't you?"

"Is it so obvious?"

"No, but it is logical. Why would you want to do this alone?"

Jack picked up a sliver-framed photo from the table beside the couch, a picture of Ben as a toddler being held by a smiling woman. She was slender, with long hair the color of Ben's and beautiful in a natural, fresh-scrubbed way. Playfulness sparkled in her eyes. "I've had the best, Quinn." His thoughts drifted off and when he spoke again it was more to himself than to me. "There is no reason in the world that I would marry again. Not after Emily."

"I can see that."

He seemed surprised that I didn't try to coax him out of his glum state. "You feel that part of your life, your God-ordained partnership, ended. You believe there's no way to replace it, so you don't plan to try."

He looked relieved to be understood. "And here I was, thinking everyone thought I was some kind of tough guy."

"I'd feel the same way if I were in your shoes. For a while, at least."

"For a while?" Jack frowned, disturbed at the idea of relinquishing any of his pain.

"Eventually I believe I'd realize that if someone loved me that much he wouldn't want me to be miserable forever."

I hurried on before Jack could respond. "I wouldn't want anyone to tell me to snap out of it or that I'd grieved two years already so it was time to move on. Grief takes the time it takes and no one should put it on a schedule."

He clasped his hands in front of him. "Grief and Loss class on Monday, cry on Tuesday and smile the rest of the week so your friends don't feel guilty about going on with their lives, you mean?"

"Is that what happened to you?"

"In a sense." He smiled weakly. "I've had to practically beat off people at work who wanted to set me up on blind dates. It seems everyone has a single sister or cousin these days."

For a man like Jack? I'll bet they do!

"I appreciate your understanding, Quinn. By not pushing me, you allow me freedom to be myself."

"From all I've seen and heard, that self is pretty amazing. Don't force another person's timetable onto yourself."

"Quinn?" His voice reminded me of Ben's. "Will you be *my* teacher, too? You're very smart. I could learn a thing or two from you."

Inexplicably I wanted to brush back the lock of hair that had fallen into his eyes and made him look so much like his son.

I went home with strangely mixed emotions. In Jack Harmon I'd met a man who, under very different circumstances, could be my soul mate. Unfortunately, he is as inaccessible as the sun over my head. I understand Maggie and her disappointments in a whole new way. Sometimes in life there is no justice.

Chapter Eighteen

Maggie's door was open when I got home. Dash was asleep on her bed and she was at the computer, staring at a screen. I bent over her shoulder to see what she was studying and unwelcome words from a Web site popped out at me.

> Imagine breaking out of your ugly cocoon! Escape those beauty trouble spots that prevent you from becoming all you can be. That's what our newest theme show can do for you. Unleash the beauty now hidden by correctable flaws. Experience the best in dental, medical and cosmetic breakthroughs, put your hair in the hands of well-known professionals and your wardrobe into the expert care of dressers to the stars. Learn about the inner you. Show your real face to the world.

I skipped to the bottom of the page. "Interviews and auditions will be held…"

"Talk about something that defeats its whole purpose! Making people feel good about themselves for a minute and then pitting them against each other in a beauty contest that will make them insecure again. Have you ever heard anything so silly?"

Maggie remained silent.

"You can see now why I'm not having anything to do with it. If you don't feel good about yourself going in, makeup and a new hairdo aren't going to fix anything. Of course, makeup companies would go broke if they depended on me for sales."

"I don't blame you, Quinn. I understand why you wouldn't want to be the hostess of this show." Maggie's voice was so soft and sure that I felt a rush of relief.

"You do? Good. I thought for a moment you might want to apply for the job."

Maggie turned her typing chair away from the computer and stared at me incredulously. "Me? Don't be silly. I'd never get a job like that. It takes someone who looks like you. Quinn, I want to be a *contestant*."

Her face brightened with pathetic hope. "It's my chance, don't you see? I could get rid of the bump in my nose and have some fat liposuctioned from my thighs. It would make all the difference in both my modeling career and personal life."

Bump in her nose? Fat on her thighs? That made as much sense as announcing she was going to have fur waxed off her back. She has no bumps, no fat and no fur.

"You can't, Maggie. They're looking for people

who have a cocoon to emerge *from*. You are already a butterfly."

I pushed back the thought of smarmy Frank jumping for joy at the chance to "ugly-up" Maggie with ill-fitting clothes and poor hair and makeup and then, by restoring her to normal, turning her into a beauty. I wouldn't put it past him. He'd do it for ratings. Eddie was aboveboard but Frank…I wouldn't put much past him.

Maggie looked at me with a serene smile at the corners of her lips. "Too late. I already have. I just got the e-mail. I'm supposed to be at the hotel at ten tomorrow for an interview."

"I'm going to throw up." After Maggie had left for her interview, Pete sat in my kitchen holding his head in his hands as Flash frantically licked Pete's arm, trying to comfort him.

Finally I took pity on Flash and tempted him into the other room with a doggy treat so that he would settle down and watch *The Andy Griffith Show* with Dash.

"There is no use talking to her anymore, anyway," I said when I returned. "She's turned a deaf ear to us."

"My wonderful idea for you is now an official disaster," Pete muttered morosely to himself. "Why did I ever tell you anything about this television show?"

"Beats me." I patted him on the back. "It isn't your fault. You believed it would be good for me. We couldn't have predicted that Maggie would get it into her head to be a contestant any more than we could have foreseen her breakup with Randy or the lost jobs. It's crazy, Pete, and you can't predict crazy."

"I'm going to start photographing flowers and birds," he announced resolutely. "No more models. No more human beings. I'm shooting only stuff that is content the way it is—mountains, deer and geraniums. I want nothing more to do with people who think that if they are prettier, thinner, thicker, wider, narrower, taller or shorter, life would be better for them. No more models—just horses, fence posts, lakes and a soup can or two thrown in for good measure."

"Andy Warhol already used that idea. Besides, you are too good at what you do to give it up. You can't help it that Maggie refuses to listen to us."

"I tried to suggest that the length to which she is going and the importance she's placing on her own looks are prideful and vain. She's fixated," Pete concluded. "Doesn't it say somewhere that obsession with beauty comes dangerously close to idolatry?"

"Nothing fazes her. She's got a one-track mind and that track leads straight to *Chrysalis*."

"At least we can count on Eddie to send her home again," Pete said. "He's a straight shooter."

"Straight shooter or not, I wouldn't depend on that. Frank might see Maggie as an opportunity to make the show more interesting."

"Nah, even Frank wouldn't do that." Worry creased Pete's expressive face. "Would he?"

"If he does, Maggie's going to need protection. Frank would happily carve Maggie up and put her back together backward for ratings."

"I'm going to call him," Pete announced, and headed for the phone.

It seemed like forever until he returned to the kitchen.

"Did you talk to him?" I pounced on Pete when he returned to the room.

"Eddie wasn't there. He's gone until tomorrow."

"Who were you talking to? I cleaned three cupboards while you were in the other room."

Pete flushed until he looked like he'd had a nasty experience in a faulty tanning bed.

"Kristy answered the phone. We talked awhile, that's all."

"Forty-five minutes."

"We have a lot to catch up on."

"You still have feelings for her."

He glared at me venomously. "Quinn, you know absolutely nothing about this."

"Of course I do. I know that when you try to keep something from me, the tip of your nose turns pink. It's been that way ever since we were kids. It's cherry colored right now so this must be a biggie."

"I thought you were annoying as a child but you are much worse now." Pete turned away. "It's amazing. The older you get, the more maddening you get. I certainly don't want to live next to you in the nursing home."

"You're still in love with her, aren't you?"

I knew by the way his neck flushed and his head drooped forward that the answer was yes.

"And she doesn't return those feelings."

He turned around and I saw how miserable he was.

"I made a mistake when I broke up with Kristy. Eddie says she never married because of me, but she's obviously not interested now."

To my surprise, Pete looked me straight in the eye and said, "If that kind of relationship ever comes along for you, Quinn, don't blow it like I did."

Chapter Nineteen

I stood at the front door of Jack's house but hesitated to ring the bell. I wasn't due here for another hour but couldn't go home because Maggie was there. I've been praying for patience and wisdom to deal with her but am still feeling pretty short in both departments. Going to Pete's is no better. He is busy reproaching himself for this ridiculous situation and mooning over Kristy. It's depressing there, too.

When I pushed the bell and no one answered, I turned back toward my car. They were out. I would do lesson plans until they returned.

I was halfway down the sidewalk when the front door opened. Jack was well turned out and elegant in a good-fitting suit and a tie that probably cost more than my entire outfit. He glanced at his watch and then at me.

"I'm sorry. I thought you weren't going to be here for an hour yet. I'll go get Ben."

"I'm early. I just didn't know where else to go."

"Then you must be in exactly the right place. Come in."

"It's silly," I said as I moved toward the dining-room table where Ben and I do our lessons, "but I needed a little sanity today and this seemed like a good place to come and find it." I glanced around. "Is Ben sleeping?"

"No. He's at Nathan's house. I just got home from the office. They wanted to do their homework together. I took it as a sign that Ben's feeling better so I let him go."

"Don't pick him up yet. I've got lesson plans to complete for next week and I can review what we're going to cover today."

Without warning, Jack's long, lean fingers engulfed mine. "Leave the books. I'd like some adult conversation for a change."

I stepped forward, caught my foot on an area rug and pitched clumsily into his arms. With my nose buried in the front of his pristine shirt, I breathed in the heady fragrances of soap and cologne. Now not only were my feet not working, my head was also spinning. My heart did a two-step in my chest.

"Are you okay?" He set me upright and peered into my face. His eyes, so close to mine, were alive with concern and amusement. His lashes were long and dusky and I had the wild notion to touch them to see if they were real. I've been a model much too long, I reminded myself, living in a world where fake eyelashes are the norm.

And his lips…they were dangerous to think about in the mood I was in.

"I tripped."

"You have to be more careful." He reached to gently wipe a strand of hair from my eyes. His touch was gossamer against my skin. "Neither Ben nor I want you injured."

He was completely unaware of the turmoil he set up inside me. "You are too important to us." As we sat together on the couch, he rubbed my arm with the back of his hand.

My mind went to a place where Jack and I could share moments such as these as often as we pleased. It was a dangerous place to tread. And a hopeless one.

"Want to tell me about it?" He was so close I could feel his breath on my cheek.

"What makes you think I have something to tell?"

"You arrived on my doorstep early and were willing to sit in your car rather than leave. You are so distracted that you fell flat on your face at my feet. It's out of character for you, Quinn."

"Thank you for your observations, Sherlock. I'll take them into consideration."

"I'm a good listener," he offered.

"I'll bet you are."

"Want to try me?" Before I realized what he was about to do, he put his arm around me and tucked me into the curve of his body. I felt the muscles of his chest and was engulfed again in the scents of aftershave and soap. Involuntarily, I leaned into his comforting strength. It felt like home.

"My roommate is losing her mind, her grip on reality and maybe even her faith. She's had some big disappointments lately and she isn't thinking rationally. Besides that, she thinks she's getting too over-the-hill for her career. Our friend Pete blames himself for a harebrained idea she came up with this week and he's feeling guilty."

The story spilled out of me like water gushing from a hydrant, but when I was done I felt the load lift. Sharing it had brought it to the light of day where the sun could evaporate the ache. "I feel sick about the whole thing and there's nothing I can do about it."

He held me near him and I had no will to resist. "You are a uniquely compassionate woman. It's difficult to watch people you love be in pain. No one knows that that better than I."

His wife. His son.

I dug in my pocket for a tissue and blew my nose. "I'm sorry for whining. After what you've been through…"

He tipped my chin upward, forcing me to look into his eyes. "Hurt is hurt, Quinn. Don't discount what's going on in your life because it's not what happened in mine."

I felt more than heard him sigh.

I fought the impulse to caress his cheek and to stroke away the tight muscle in his jaw. "Is something wrong with Ben?" I remained very still, feeling that if I moved, this moment of confidence would be broken.

"No, not Ben." His faint smile turned crooked and faded. "Oddly enough, it's me. Since we're telling tales on ourselves, may I share something with you?"

My hand tightened over his in telegraphed permission.

"My wife has been gone over two years. When Emily died, friends, relatives and neighbors poured through this house. I found food in my refrigerator, fresh sheets on the bed, fruit baskets on the counters until it looked like we ran an orchard. Mail came by the sack.

"On the first anniversary of her passing a few people came by to see if I wanted a diversion or company. I got letters from family and someone sent Ben and I tickets to a ball game. Something to divert us on the day his mother died, I suppose. Oddly, no one seemed to want to talk about Emily. Our family and friends have now moved beyond their loss and feel Ben and I should, too."

"Have you?" I asked gently, already sure of the answer.

He squirmed, making me slip toward him on the sofa. I made no attempt to move away. Even if I'd wanted to, my body was too content beside his.

He didn't answer my question directly. "Ben's doing well. A counselor has helped him a great deal. He talks to his grandparents about it and to me. He loves his mother but accepts that she's no longer here. He's moved on and I haven't." He paused, genuinely flummoxed that it was he who was not the high achiever, the head of the pack.

"Have *you* got anyone to talk to? Someone who would just listen?"

"Someone who hasn't tried to fix me in the process? Not really." His expression softened. "No, Quinn, I don't believe I do know anyone who is willing to just listen."

"I'm a good listener too."

His lips tipped in a smile and he gave me an appreciative hug that didn't last nearly long enough. "It might be an onerous job to take on."

"Let me be the judge of that."

When he spoke, he said something I had not expected. "I've met a lot of beautiful women since my wife died."

He saw the startled expression on my face and laughed. "Sympathy casseroles came pouring into the house. It seemed every single woman I'd ever known turned up on the doorstep with food and a listening ear."

Ouch. A new handsome and single guy in town? Is that what had motivated them?

"Let's just say I made it my policy not to encourage anyone to think there was anything to be had from me other than appreciation, but it did make me skittish."

"I'm sure."

"I got in the habit of keeping everyone at arm's length," he admitted thoughtfully, "and until I met you, it didn't seem like much of a problem."

"Oh?" My best policy was going to be silence. I could tell that already.

"But with you...." He looked deep into my eyes and it was as if he were trying to see my soul. "There's something else going on."

"Something other than using a casserole as bait?"

He laughed out loud. "You've nailed it, Quinn."

I didn't say anything and when he spoke, he was musing to himself, not to me. "When I think about you I don't see Emily in my mind, only you." He looked out the window into the distance as if he were seeing something I couldn't. "It's a relief, Quinn. When I'm with you the pain is not there."

He frowned a little. "Should I feel guilty about that?"

"Would you want Ben to continue to hurt forever?"

"Of course not, I—I see what you mean." He pulled

me closer and we sat together quietly sharing the moment. Something had changed inside of Jack. What, I wasn't sure, but I think it was for the better.

When the phone rang, he let the answering machine pick up.

Linda's voice chimed into the room. "Listen, Jack, the boys are having such a wonderful time that I don't want to interrupt them. I can't remember if you need Ben home at any certain time but if not, I'll just keep him here until you come by. No hurry. They've been having sea battles in the kitchen sink and now that they've drowned all the action figures, they're doing triage. Take your time. Bye."

Neither of us moved. Suddenly we had all the time in the world.

In the still of the large room, curled on the couch that threatened to swallow us both, we talked. Or, more correctly, Jack talked and I listened.

Chapter Twenty

Eventually we moved from the couch to the kitchen where Jack brewed coffee and made sandwiches.

Emotion is a hungry business. We polished off a plate of sandwiches, a bag of chips, most of a package of cookies and a pint of Rocky Road ice cream.

Linda called at six to ask if Ben could stay for dinner, leaving us to continue our get-to-know-each-other marathon into the evening.

Somehow in the course of this extended and intimate afternoon, he had become the listener again, with Maggie and *Chrysalis* the topics.

"She's on a collision course with disaster. What am I going to do about her?"

"She's a grown woman. She can do what she wants."

"Makeover shows have made women cavalier about cosmetic surgery. They see condensed into quick shots what is actually hours in a surgical suite and weeks of recovery—if all goes well, that is.

"People choose from a menu of improvements like they order at a deli. 'I'll have a tummy tuck, something done with my jowls and do my eyes while you're at it. Oh, yes, my thighs are too thick and my teeth are uneven. Why don't we take care of it all at once?" I shuddered and Jack rubbed my arm. Even the fire he'd built to ward off the coolness of the fall air didn't help. The source of my chill was purely internal.

"It gives me the creeps. Maggie stands at the bathroom mirror sucking in her cheeks and asking me if I think she'd look better if they removed some fat from her face. She'd never even *thought* of that until Frank suggested it to her."

"This Frank is quite a salesman."

"Frank is a manipulator. I've watched him since day one. Pete said as much but now I've seen it for myself. Pete is beginning to suspect Frank bought her onto the show because he was attracted to her, not because she needed help. He is always thinking of reasons to cozy up to the women on the set and he's relentless once he decides to pursue one of them."

"I take it you know from experience?" Jack frowned at the idea.

"I'm usually tutoring around the lunch hour so it is easy to say no to him. Several evenings Pete was at my house and picked up the phone when he called. I guess he finally got the idea that I wasn't available— to him, at least."

"I wonder why he's a partner in the business."

"He knows how to pump up ratings, for one thing. And he's very good at what he does. I'm afraid he's going to bring up the idea of a nose job and chin reduction for Maggie next. He wouldn't care a bit if she was unrecognizable by the time he was through. It would be quite a triumph if he could made a beautiful woman into a spectacular one."

Jack set a cup of steaming hot cider in front of me. "It's unethical for a doctor to suggest procedures that might distort a patient's face or body."

"But Frank isn't a doctor and I'm not sure he has any ethics. Or maybe I'm being too hard on Frank. Perhaps it's Maggie I'm most upset with for buying into this." I scraped my fingers through the hair tumbling around my shoulders. "I feel so helpless."

"Maybe you *should* be on that television set," Jack commented casually, "to protect her. If they still haven't filled the hostess spot they may be waiting for you to change your mind. You said they're still pressuring your friend Pete to talk you into it."

Would a voice of reason be heard over the circus atmosphere developing around this show? If Maggie went ahead with everything Frank suggested, it would be a disaster. It was *surgery,* not the trip to the beauty parlor as my roommate seemed to think. Sometimes things go wrong in surgery. Sometimes people come out damaged—or dead.

"It goes against everything in me to encourage this."

Jack absently played with the fingers of my left hand as it lay on the table. I did nothing to pull it away.

"If I could convince these women of their real, innate beauty, their beauty in God's eyes, maybe they wouldn't embrace such radical measures. Would that make me some sort of undercover agent trying to destroy the show's concept?"

"You told me the show is about all kinds of beauty, inner as well as outer. They want you because you have something more, something they can't quite define that goes beyond medical advancements."

"So they say."

He picked up a banana from the fruit bowl on the table and spoke into it like a microphone. "And to what do you attribute your inner beauty, Ms. Hunter?" he intoned, sounding remarkably like Frank.

"God, of course. You can't shine from the inside out unless you've got the light."

"And you have that light?"

Suddenly an idea actually did spark in my brain. I jumped to my feet and dashed for my cell phone.

"What are you doing?"

"I'm calling Eddie. If he is serious about letting me share what real beauty means to me then he just might have a hostess for his show."

"Besides—" I covered the phone with my hand as it rang "—I don't want to take any chances that Maggie or any of the others go over the deep end."

A voice rumbled into my ear.

"Hello, Eddie? It's Quinn Hunter. I'd like to make an appointment to talk with you…."

"You are going to do *what?*" Pete stared at me in dumbfounded exasperation.

Eddie Bessett, on the other hand, looked calm and

thoughtful. "So you will do the show if we give the internal beauty parts at least equal time with the external. Stuff like poise, self-respect…"

"Faith."

"Only if it is genuine, Quinn. I don't want this to be some kind of revival show."

"That's been the sticking point all along," I pointed out patiently. "You say you want to show inner transformation as well as the outer one. My roommate has indicated that she's had consultations with cosmetic surgeons, dentists and hairstylists. Eddie, you have a contestant who is willing to cut off her little toes so that she can fit into prettier shoes! It sounds like you are chronicling insanity, not transformation."

Eddie turned to Pete with a sour look. "I blame you for this."

"Wha-what'd I do?"

"If you hadn't brought Quinn here in the first place, I wouldn't have gotten so stuck on the idea of having her in the show."

"And you'd have the same repetitive show that we've already seen," Pete answered.

"What if she talks them all out of having anything done? Frank's already complaining."

"If Quinn talks through the process with each of these women, they'll become real people to the audience, not stick figures to watch for a few minutes before turning to the nightly news. The audience will recognize themselves in the contestants. That's what made your show *Hide-and-Seek* such a hit. People identified with others like themselves. I remember watching the show and wondering where I would look for the treasure."

"I saw the show once, too," I added. "All I could think about was how I'd spend the money."

"You only watched the show once?"

"Well, it *was* the end of the season when Pete told me about it."

Eddie looked steadily at me. "What made you change your mind about *Chrysalis?*"

"My friend Jack suggested that perhaps it was God's will that I do this so initially I prayed for wisdom and discernment about the show. I was sure His answer would be 'No, don't be ridiculous' but it wasn't. He's been surprisingly quiet on the subject."

Pete's eyebrows shot upward at the mention of Jack.

"Jack suggested that being with Maggie on the show might be the right thing to do."

"And what did God say to that?"

Eddie meant to be sarcastic, but I smiled at him. "I expected Him to put all sorts of stops in my way, but it hasn't happened. My growing sense is that it is what I'm supposed to be doing. God is always reaching for His children. If they're watching television, then that's where He'll go to find them."

The strange look on Eddie's face almost made me laugh. He hadn't expected that. God and reality television?

"Be forewarned, Eddie, if you want me to do this, you'll be putting a Christian woman on air."

"I said no sermons."

"I'm not hiding my light under a bushel basket, either."

Eddie assumed a pained expression.

Pete looked at me askance and mouthed, *What do you think you're doing?*

Putting out a fleece like Gideon, I realized. If, after what I'd said, Eddie still let me on the show…

"Frank already thinks I'm nuts. He's complained all along about the 'internal beauty' thing. I'm the one who thought it was a good idea," Eddie said. "Well, if God wants it, who am I to stand in His way? Just don't get preachy on me, Quinn."

A sense of calm washed over me and I smiled serenely at Eddie. "I won't have to, Eddie. Faith speaks for itself."

Chapter Twenty-One

"Are you *sure* you don't mind that I took the job, Maggie?"

"It was offered to you first, Quinn. Of course I don't mind. It will be nice to have you on the set, reassuring."

The sun shone through Pete's many windows and I was tempted, as always, to look for the sunglasses in my purse.

"Are you nervous?" Maggie asked.

Nervous enough to change your mind?

"This is what I want to do, if that's what you mean."

"But you have doubts?" I knew she'd begun to mistrust Frank's motives too but there was no way she'd admit it.

"Don't try to put words in my mouth, Quinn. I know you think I'm crazy to consider this but I have to do *something*."

"Have you considered believing in yourself or praying for guidance? Unless you change the way you *think,* you will never *feel* good about yourself."

"I have prayed, but I haven't heard any answers. Maybe He isn't listening."

"He's listening but when the answer does come, you have to trust it."

"She's scared," I told Pete when Maggie left the room. "Petrified. And still determined to go through with it."

"I should never have opened my mouth." Pete absently petted Flash's head as the dog rested it on Pete's knee. Flash instinctively knows when Pete is upset and won't leave his side. If Maggie and I are Pete's two best friends, Flash is his third.

"Yet you got to see Kristy Bessett again by reconnecting with her brother."

"A fat lot of good that has done. She's been totally aloof. She hates me." Pete looked as huggable as a teddy bear as he slouched miserably on his couch. "I deserve it."

"Could be," I said cheerfully, "but I doubt it. They're taping an interview with Maggie and me this afternoon. She's supposed to explain why she wanted to be a *Chrysalis* contestant. Want to come along? Eddie won't mind."

"I might as well. I won't get anything done here."

"My part of the show is in 'conversational' format, like I might have with my best friend. They want me to ask the contestants how they think it will change their lives and if they really want to go through with it. To build tension, I suppose.

"Pete, remind me again why I'm doing this."

"To save your best friend from committing the biggest mistake of her life?"

"Oh, that."

"And you are independent. Eddie likes that whether he admits it or not. You'll do whatever you please and Eddie enjoys an element of danger and surprise. He is partial to bombshells being dropped."

Pete looked at me with genuine admiration. "You know, Quinn, the guy that ends up with you will have his hands full." I looked at Pete askance and he hurried to add, "in a good way, of course. A very good way."

The studio looks more like someone's living room than a set for a reality-television show. Pete took in the large inviting chairs and ottomans, end tables decorated with flowers and dimmed lights. "I thought it would be more antiseptic."

A dark-haired man I'd seen around the set the past two days, with headphones encircling the back of his neck, a walkie-talkie strapped to his belt and sheaf of papers in his hand, smiled at us. "It was going to be, but once Quinn came on board Eddie decided to switch things up. It's changed the flavor of the entire show."

The fellow was tan, broad shouldered and obviously spent a lot of time at the gym. But what was more noticeable were his uneven features. He must have once been a boxer. His nose and jaw were slightly rearranged on his face. His smile was broad and friendly and his teeth white, but there were far too many of them. They overlapped each other at odd angles and his front tooth displayed a large chip.

He stuck out his hand to Pete. "Sam Waters. I'm Eddie and Frank's jack-of-all-trades, the silent partner in B & B Productions. I just came in a couple days ago. I coproduce, direct, run for food, act as official greeter, whatever needs to be done."

"You're the one Eddie and Kristy talk about." A smile poured across Pete's features as he pumped Sam's hand. "Eddie says great things about you." Then he remembered me. "You probably already know Quinn."

Sam took my hand and leaned over it as if he might kiss it. "I'm so glad to officially meet you. You're the one putting this show on a new track."

Sam might not be traditionally handsome, but he certainly oozed charm.

"Thanks to you, they're not going to do just frantic shots of the contestants at all stages of their transformation—with a trainer, obsessing before liposuction, blah, blah, blah. They think that you can bring out more of what the contestants are thinking and feeling. They want you to ask the hard questions, the emotional ones."

"Shades of Barbara Walters," Pete muttered.

"That's it exactly!" Sam smiled approvingly at him. As unlovely as his features might be, he radiated kindness and sincerity. He was impossible not to like.

"Frankly, I like this format better." Sam lowered his voice. "This way we can't predict exactly what the contestants will decide to do. Like free will or something."

"It doesn't seem like Frank's kind of show," Pete commented.

"It isn't. It's mine. Look at my ugly mug," Sam said cheerfully. "I used to be a boxer. My face got reshuffled and my nose moved around so many times I felt I was working for Allied Van Lines, but I'm still the same guy that I always was. My sister says I have an 'interesting' face and that's good enough for me."

I wanted to throw my arms around him and hug him. Finally! Sanity in an insane world.

On our way back to Pete's after the taping he said, "Do you remember my dad's sister Alyce?"

"Of course. I loved your aunt Alyce."

"What do you remember most about her?"

I tried to picture Pete's aunt in my mind. "She always wore an apron and had candy in her pockets."

"What else?"

"She was always smiling. When I came over she'd beam like a lighthouse. She made me feel that I had given her the biggest gift on earth—my company." Memories began flooding back. "And that time I fell off her porch and scraped my knee? She picked me up and rocked me on the porch swing until I quit crying. Frankly, I kept whimpering longer than I needed to just because I didn't want her to put me down."

"Did you think she was beautiful?"

"Of course! She was the most amazing, kind person. I'll never forget her."

"But did you think she was beautiful?"

My first response was to say yes. As a child, I'd always wanted to grow up to be just like her.

And yet... I recalled her more-than-ample bosom and her thick sturdy legs. Alyce was a big woman, nearly six feet tall and rawboned. Her hair was mousy brown and she wore it pulled back into a tight bun. The style highlighted the scars on her temple and forehead from a childhood tangle with a barbed-wire fence.

Alyce told me once that she looked like her father rather than her dainty mother. "That is not the luckiest thing for a young girl. I wanted to be feminine looking like my mother, but that husband of mine insists he likes me just the way I am." She'd twinkled at me conspiratorially. "He even says I should gain a couple pounds. I love that man."

"Physically beautiful? Not really, but when I picture her in my mind she's so lovely."

"A lot like Sam?" Pete asked cagily.

"Exactly. There is something special about Sam, isn't there? His openness, his confidence…"

"I spent some time with Eddie while you were busy this afternoon. Eddie tells me Sam is a big-time believer and that Sam's faith is what makes him like he is. He told Eddie that until he was right with God inside, there was no use changing his looks or having surgery to repair what boxing did to him. And now that he is, he doesn't feel the need to do more. Cool, huh?"

Cool, indeed.

Lord, you've gathered us all together for a purpose. Me, Pete, Eddie, Kristy, Maggie, the other contestants, Sam…and even Frank although I can't imagine why. What is going on? I felt Your leading to accept this job and now I have no idea what to do with it. I'm on the underside of this weaving, Lord, and it just looks like a bunch of tangled knots to me.

Chapter Twenty-Two

"**D**id somebody die or did you just win the Kentucky Derby?" Pete stared at the bouquet on my kitchen table. It was a lavish mix of red, yellow, peach and white roses, extravagant lilies and lush greens. He picked up the card that I had propped on the cut-crystal vase. *Thanks for listening. Jack.*

He whistled through his teeth. "You must be quite a listener. Do you know how much roses are going for these days?"

"Been sending lots of roses yourself lately, have you, Pete?"

He flushed to the roots of his hair.

So he *is* trying to romance Kristy Bessett back into his life. Score one for me.

"No fair," he whined.

"I'm glad. I like her. Why didn't you tell me?"

"Because if I'm going to fall on my face I want to do

it in private, thank you very much. And don't change the subject. These are your flowers."

"No, this is the subject. I want to hear about Kristy."

Pete made a face at me and left.

I changed into pencil-thin leggings and a long flowing tunic, fluffed my hair and applied some lipstick. Then I picked up my briefcase and headed for the Harmon house.

Butterflies, they're everywhere.

"Why are cocoons so ugly and butterflies so beautiful?" Ben asked as he stared at the colored photos I'd given him.

"We'll cover that tomorrow. Tonight you can read up on butterflies in this book."

"I'd rather you just told me."

"I'm sure you would, but you wouldn't learn everything you needed to know if I did that. Sometimes you have to struggle a little for something good to come out of it."

"What do you mean?"

"Take the butterfly, for example. It struggles to make its way out of its cocoon, but when it does, see how lovely it is?"

"It would be just as pretty if we helped it out," Ben maintained. "And I'd be just as smart if you told me the answers and I didn't have to read them."

"That's not quite true. If someone 'helps' a butterfly by releasing it from its cocoon and doesn't allow it to work its way out by itself, it might not be able to stretch out its wings properly to dry. Unless it does its own work, it is weak and misshapen and will die."

Just like all of us, I mused, especially like Maggie, who wants quick answers to difficult questions.

Jack met me as I came out of Ben's room. "I think you're going to make him into a biologist yet."

"I love your little boy, Jack. He is a bright spot in my day. Are you considering sending him back to school soon?"

"Neither of us wants you to quit coming to the house, Quinn. Ben told me that he thinks it would be 'just great' if you were his full-time teacher."

"He needs the socialization. If he's feeling well enough he should—"

Jack stopped in the middle of the hallway and looked *down* into my eyes, a very pleasant sensation for a tall woman. "Our lives are different since you started coming here."

"I'm surprised you don't want to get rid of me before I cause any more havoc."

"I don't think we'll ever want to do that."

Unexpectedly, Jack bent his head and tenderly brushed my lips with his.

We both froze, paralyzed by what had just happened.

"I'm sorry, Quinn. I didn't plan to…I don't know what came over me. I forgot myself for a moment."

What he really meant to say, I realized, was that during the impulsive kiss, he had forgotten Emily.

I followed Jack into the kitchen to gather my things. Without speaking, I picked up my purse and sweater.

"Quinn, I don't know what to say."

Jack looked so worried that I burst out laughing.

"You didn't kick my crutches out from under me, you know? You did something wonderful."

"Wonderful? You're too kind. I'm a little out of practice." He put his hand on my shoulder. "Sit down. I'd like to talk to you."

"Jack, it's fine. Like I said, it was nice. Sweet. Flattering."

He raked his fingers through his hair. "Then what's wrong with me? Why do I feel like I just betrayed my wife?"

"You know on one level that it is time to move on," I offered gently, "but you're not sure how to begin—or even if you want to."

"Losing Emily was like losing a limb, Quinn. I'm plagued with phantom pain. Like the nerves in a severed foot that still send pain signals to the brain, my marriage still feels real."

He stared at me as if willing me to understand. "Emily's passing is like an amputation. I'll never get over it and I'm reminded of what's missing every day."

Chapter Twenty-Three

Life is growing more complex by the day.

Maggie is on a whirlwind tour of beauty consultants, plastic surgeons and cosmetic dentists with Frank, Sam Waters and a cameraman. Sam must be as nice a guy as Pete said because Maggie came home three days in a row quoting something Sam had said while they were together. I was beginning to like Sam more and more even though I wasn't the one spending time with him. Maggie has also been sworn to secrecy by Frank, because I am supposed to pry the details of that out of her when she and I tape our interviews. Much to my relief she has quit mentioning Randy and her unrequited love for him. It's as if he's been erased from the chalkboard of her life.

Pete moons around like a lovesick calf because Kristy does not return his calls. I alternately tell him it serves him right for dumping her so unceremoniously and give him hints for trying to win her back. So far nothing has worked. Kristy is one determined woman. She'd be perfect for Pete. Too bad she can't stand the ground he walks on.

Ben is doing fabulously and is ready to go back to school full-time. It's just as well. I've been thinking about Jack and the kiss we shared far too much. When I told Pete and Maggie, they weren't nearly as surprised about it as I thought they'd be.

"Sometimes the one involved is the last to know," Pete said mysteriously as we brooded over a family-sized pizza and a pitcher of root beer in our favorite pizza joint. Maggie, in the name of dieting, had eaten only the toppings off her share, leaving the crusts for Pete to finish off.

"You should know," Maggie commented dourly.

"What's that supposed to mean?" Pete appeared indignant.

"What do you both mean?" I looked from Pete to Maggie and back again. "Am I the only one who doesn't know what this conversation is about?"

"Clueless, clueless, clueless. You and Pete haven't got a clue about your own love lives." Maggie stole a piece of my Canadian bacon. "Pete, you are so in love with Kristy that it has turned you into a bowl of mush."

"Has not."

"Has too." Maggie stole a piece of pineapple to go with her bacon. "And you! You don't even realize it, but half the time when you're talking about Pete or Eddie you are saying Jack's name instead."

"Am not!"

"Are too."

"Aren't you the psychologist today?" Pete grumped. He grabbed my toppingless crust before I even got a bite of it. "Physician heal thyself."

"I am. That's why I'm on *Chrysalis*. Besides, I'm so over Randy." Maggie flipped her hair away from her face and I saw a bit of the old Maggie, the carefree one. "He's yesterday's news. Last week's news. Last *year's* news!"

"You got yourself into this *Chrysalis* nonsense because you thought you weren't pretty enough for Randy," Pete said. "Now you can get off the show before Frank gets a chance to have someone carve you up and put you together backward for ratings."

Then Pete made me the bug under his microscope. "And you are in some dreamy altered state most of the time because of Jack Harmon. He's everything you want in a man—except available."

"That's ridiculous!"

"You are so preoccupied that you don't even hear me talk sometimes." Maggie eyed me speculatively. If that's not a sign that you're falling for Jack Harmon, I don't know what is."

"Jack will never have another relationship. No living woman can compete with the pedestal on which he's put his former wife. In Jack's mind, Emily is perfect and will be for infinity. Even if he were interested in me— and he's not—I couldn't live up to her memory."

I felt a crushing heaviness on my chest and put my head in my hands. "You guys are messing with my mind. I'm so mixed up."

"Join the crowd." Pete swilled down the last of his

soda. "Since it's apparent to everyone else, I guess I'd better accept it. I am crazy about Kristy and I'm furious with myself. I've tried to make it up to her that I was a jerk, but she is completely unresponsive. It's like trying to melt stone." His voice softened. "A beautiful, mysterious, gentle, sweet, amazing stone."

"If that's not love I don't know what is," Maggie said smugly. "I told you guys you were clueless about your own feelings."

"That's the pot calling the kettle black." Pete turned on her.

"I don't know what you mean." Maggie drew her shoulders back and looked at him haughtily. "I have simply put Randy behind me, that is all."

"So who is it?" The words came out of my mouth unbidden.

"What makes you think that there has to be someone else on my radar in order for me to get over Randy?"

"It's your modus operandi, Maggie. Have you ever quit obsessing about one guy until you've spotted another?"

"Am I so insecure that you think I can't go it alone?"

Pete and I nodded vehemently and Maggie threw up her hands. "Okay, so I am insecure. I can't hide that from anyone now that I was fool enough to become a contestant on *Chrysalis*."

Pete and I both jumped on that. "Fool?" we chimed.

Maggie clamped her lips together like a vise. "I'm not saying another word. Frank would have my scalp if he knew I was talking to Quinn about this. Don't ask me anymore."

"But you didn't promise anyone you wouldn't talk

about Randy or why you lost interest in him," Pete pointed out. "Who is it, Mags? Who's the new guy?"

She reddened to the roots of her hair. "I won't say."

"Why not?"

"Because it is crazy. I don't understand the attraction myself and it won't last." Maggie looked truly baffled. "He's no one I ever expected to care about."

Much to my and Pete's dismay, that's the last she would say on the subject.

Chapter Twenty-Four

"Thanks for letting me come along. My boredom quotient is off the charts today." Maggie tilted her seat back and Dash, in the backseat of my car, licked her forehead before poking his black gumdrop nose out the partially open car window again.

"No problem. I'll just drop this workbook off with Ben Harmon and then we'll have lunch."

"So I'm finally going to meet this little boy you talk about…and his father."

"Don't get your hopes up. If they aren't there, I'll leave the book by the entry."

"They'd better be there. I've got to meet this man…er…child for myself."

Sometimes no comment is the wisest answer.

Maggie was in luck. Jack's van was in the driveway. Ben had the door open and was digging through the cubbyhole on the passenger side. When we drove up and he saw it was me, his eyes lit and a delighted grin spread over his features.

As I got out of the car he threw his arms around my waist. "I didn't know we had school today!"

"We don't. It's Saturday. I brought you that book I promised to you."

Ben's gaze moved to Maggie. "Hi, I'm Ben."

"Hi, I'm Quinn's friend, Maggie."

He solemnly shook her hand as if it were the most important thing he'd ever done. "I'm glad to meet you, Maggie."

I watched my friend begin to melt. Ben has that effect on people.

"Is your dad around?"

"He's on the phone." He wrinkled his nose. "He's been on it all morning."

Ben turned to Maggie and held out his hand. "Want to see my room?"

She looked at me nonplussed.

"Sure," I answered for her. "I'll go with you. You have to see Ben's volcano."

"I'll blow it up for you, Maggie. It's cool."

We followed Ben to his room, a veritable museum of delights for ten-year-old boys. There was something new since I'd been here last. Paper butterflies drifted lazily from the ceiling.

"Dad got me a book of butterflies. I colored them and he hung them up. I like butterflies." Ben took Maggie by the hand and pulled her toward his volcano. "Quinn helped us with this. Dad and I were making a big mess and…"

I heard Jack come up the stairs and slipped out of the room to meet him.

"Hi, did you bring the book?" he greeted me. His hair was tousled, his jeans and rumpled sweatshirt appeared to have spent the night on the bedroom floor and his feet were bare. On him, it's a look I like.

"I left it on the table downstairs. Ben insisted Maggie see his room."

"That might take a while. Come on. I've got coffee on." He touched my elbow and steered me toward the kitchen.

There, he stared at me like a hungry man looking at an apple pie. "It's been too long since I last saw you, Quinn."

I stopped myself from saying it hadn't been all that long. It was nice to have been missed.

There, Jack absently put some small lumps of dough on the table with a butter dish and some knives.

"The Food Channel failed me," he said by way of apology. "I think if there are any left I'll have enough hockey pucks to take me through the winter."

I took one of the lumps and broke it open. "It's not the Food Channel that failed you. It was the yeast. It must have been old."

"Yeast gets old?" He sounded surprised. "Nobody on the Food Channel told me that."

"Are we interrupting your plans for the morning?"

"No. Sometimes I lift weights or play basketball at the gym if Ben's got something to do. Otherwise we just hang out."

"You sound a little down in the mouth today." I surprised myself with that bit of honesty. "Sad."

He didn't seem taken aback by my comment. "Sad? I don't know. Regretful? Maybe. Angry? Sometimes."

"It's hard for you that Ben can't share in physical activities with you."

"Ironic, isn't it? Sports have always been a huge part of my life. They've been my sanity, sometimes. Yet Ben will never experience it as I have."

He looked pensive. "Even though he's the one with the 'condition' he is, in many ways, healthier than the rest of us. Sometimes I wonder who is taking care of whom around here."

Ben and Maggie entered the kitchen holding hands. Ben chattered happily but Maggie looked bewildered and perplexed, as if she'd just seen or heard something that had shaken her.

"Mags?"

"She really likes my room, Quinn. We talked about butterflies." He pulled on Maggie's hand. "Right?"

She nodded but still looked numb.

Oblivious, Ben turned to his father. "Maggie says that Quinn likes flea markets."

"She does, does she?" Jack looked amused and reached to shake Maggie's hand.

"And she goes to them on Saturdays."

"And the point is?" Jack got up and poured Maggie some coffee.

"That you should take her."

The room grew suddenly still.

"Ben, I don't think it's appropriate that you make plans for Quinn."

"She'd like it." Ben spun to face me. "Wouldn't you?"

"I…ah…well…"

"See? She didn't say no."

Ben turned to me. The innocence in his expression pulled at my heart. "I can go to Nathan's. Nathan's mom says Dad needs to get out more. Will you take him out?"

He was looking out for his dad again.

"She'd love to." We all turned to look at Maggie who'd roused herself from her daze long enough to join forces with Ben. "Pick her up at one."

"What did you do that for?" I demanded when we were back in the car, away from Ben's pleased gloat and Jack's bemused expression. "You two set us up on a date without even asking!"

"You'll never do it on your own. You wouldn't ask him out and Jack's obviously paralyzed by his own memories. Somebody has to set a fire under you. Otherwise you'll never wake up and see that you're falling in love with him."

"Now your fantasies have gone too far."

"Have they?" Maggie eyed me speculatively and I felt a strange burning blush working its way through my body.

"Did you plan this nonsense while you were examining Ben's butterflies?"

"No. I just saw where Ben was going and jumped on board. That is one amazing little kid. He's a lesson to the rest of us about how to approach life, that's for sure."

"What do you mean?"

Maggie frowned. "I'm not sure yet."

After that odd answer she grew quiet and we drove the rest of the way home in silence.

At one o'clock I found myself staring out the window, wondering if Jack would actually show up. Jack and I had parted in a haze of embarrassment and I had no idea if he'd taken his son seriously. I'd be shocked if he came and disappointed if he didn't.

I wasn't disappointed.

Jack pulled up in my driveway and came to my door with a sheepish expression on his handsome face. "Why do I feel I've been tricked, manipulated and stage-managed into something I wanted to do anyway?"

"Because you have been—by two experts. And the question is, would you be going to a flea market today if they hadn't manipulated you into it?"

"No."

"Case closed." I grabbed a denim jacket off a hanger and joined Jack on the front step. "Besides, I got conned, too. All that's left to do is enjoy it."

It didn't occur to me until I was almost to Jack's vehicle that he wasn't driving his van. "Nice wheels. This certainly isn't the daddy-mobile you usually drive." I ran my finger over the finish of the low, sleek sliver Beemer.

"Ben doesn't like to ride in it. The rules are different from the van—no eating, no videos, no radio…"

"No fun?"

"I suppose not. It's a big boy's toy, not that of a ten year old."

"I see that," I practically purred as I slid into a seat that felt as if it was made of kid leather. "This is the nicest ride I've ever had to a flea market."

We pulled into a parking spot as several people walked by carrying their purchases—an old floor lamp, toys, a velvet Elvis.

"Why is everyone leaving?" Jack wondered.

"These things start early. That's when you get the really good stuff. By now the early shoppers are on their way home."

"Did we miss something wonderful?" A light breeze ruffled Jack's hair as he stared at the dozens of tents and tables spread out before us.

"Probably, but we can live without it. I only shop for a few things—vintage jewelry, silver pieces and the occasional piece of glassware." I pointed to the far corner of the tables. "There are usually some nice pieces of jewelry over there."

"Do you know what you're looking for?"

"I often shop for my mother. She's a collector and I've got a pretty good eye."

"I'll bet you do." He was checking out more than my eyes, I noticed. An unbidden shiver of pleasure ran through me. *Thank you, Ben and Maggie!*

My gratitude only grew as Jack and I explored the flea market together. More than once I reached for his hand to pull him toward one table or another and he let it go with reluctance. His wall of reserve was not down, but there were definite chinks in the mortar.

"I think dinner is in order," Jack suggested as we pulled away from the market with a small bag of treasures, a sterling silver teapot black with age, three silver teaspoons and an assortment of costume jewelry.

"Shopping makes me hungry," I offered, pleased by his suggestion.

He looked at me with a soft, warm expression. "I know just the place to go."

The Italian restaurant was tucked into the basement of a large industrial building now made into trendy lofts. The walls were original brick, the floor rough with age and use and candles filled the room with a moody, shadowy ambiance.

"A booth, please," Jack requested. The banquettes were upholstered in rich Italian tapestry and red velvet curtains encircled the space like an embrace. A tall candle guttered in an ancient wine bottle and elegant ivory linens draped the table.

As my eyes grew accustomed to the dimness, I noticed other details. Rich oil paintings, fine crystal and large baskets of warm breads on the table. "I didn't know this place existed."

"One of my clients owns it. I've wanted to come here for some time, but he told me it's not a place to come alone." He reached across the table and put his hand over mine. "Thank you for sharing the experience with me."

"My pleasure" wouldn't have said enough. It was my absolute delight.

Jack leaned against the padded back of the booth and studied me through half-closed eyes. His gaze felt smoky and mysterious as it grazed my features. A flicker of warmth grew within me.

What was he thinking? I wondered. Was it about me? Or were his thoughts with the ghost of Emily, who couldn't be here with him?

Chapter Twenty-Five

The romantic atmosphere had the opposite effect on Jack from what I'd hoped. He seemed to sink deeper and deeper into an emotional morass with every course. By the time dessert arrived, I had to say something.

"What is it, Jack? Instead of enjoying this wonderful meal, you're looking more and more miserable."

"It shows that much, huh?" He smiled with his lips but his eyes were dark, unreadable pools.

"I'm beginning to get a complex. Usually men enjoy my company."

He looked startled. "Quinn, I *love* your company. You are the first woman I've met since Emily who hasn't pressured me into anything I don't want to say or do. You're a gift, a delight. I'm sorry if I've offended you. It's just that…" And his thoughts seemed to drift away once more.

This time, however, he managed to reel them in again.

He picked up my hand and cradled it between his palms. "Going out like this is the closest I've come to what my sister calls 'moving on with my life.'" His fingers kneaded the soft dip at my wrist and sent a tremor through me.

He looked at me apologetically. "I'm sorry, Quinn. I know I need to move on with my life but I simply can't figure out how."

"Or if you'll ever want to?" I asked as gently as I could.

"'Ever' is a long time." He took his hands away from mine, leaving me feeling chilled and bereft.

"Do you want coffee, Quinn, or are you ready to go home?"

I found Pete and Maggie there, waiting for me. Pete was pouring chocolate sauce over vanilla ice cream and the dogs were watching him raptly, as usual.

"How was it?" Maggie jumped to her feet when I entered the kitchen. "Wonderful?"

"Very nice."

"*Nice?* Isn't that a word like *fine?* If something is *nice* or *fine* it's like getting an average grade in school. I want you to say it was an A plus. "

"It really was…nice. Pleasant. Enjoyable."

"I can find that much fun going to the grocery store! He's gorgeous, Quinn, as adorable as that super cute son of his. Why didn't he just sweep you away?"

"It's impossible." I sagged onto a chair. "He's already taken."

"Dating?" Pete looked up from his ice cream. "Nobody ever said that before."

"Not dating—married. Jack's been a widow for over two years, but he's still very much married to his memories. He's not ready for someone new in his life yet and may never be."

"Bummer," Pete commented. "Then you're in a fix no better than mine. Kristy won't have anything to do with me, either."

"I think we've both fallen in love with the unattainable people."

"Love, you say? Quinn, are you saying you're falling in love?"

"Does Jack know this?" Maggie dipped celery sticks into a puddle of chocolate syrup on a plate, her idea of dieting yet not depriving herself.

"He knows I love Ben, but who wouldn't? But he's still grieving for Emily. It's something very personal that he has to work out for himself. There are times when I see how much he does care for me, but there's no way I'm going to attempt to muscle my way into this life and try to banish her from his thoughts. This is something Jack has to do alone."

"And there is no chance that—"

"None whatsoever. He's said as much. He'll never marry again. He's had 'the best.'"

Maggie whistled through her teeth. "Now that's tough competition."

The vision of me as a tight-lipped spinster schoolteacher began to loom in my mind. She wore a starched white blouse, a black skirt and shoes like those worn by the Wicked Witch of the West. Her hair was sparse and gray and her mouth pinched like she'd been sucking on a pickle for thirty years. Would that, could that, someday, be me?

I would have to revise that vision if it was going to work for me, I decided. First I'd give my pathetic spinster new shoes.

With Ben and Nathan both back in school for the past three weeks, I was left with no excuse whatsoever to be hanging around their neighborhood except, of course, for my friendship with Nathan's mother, Linda.

"I've missed having you around," Linda told me as she poured me a cup of coffee. "What's new?"

Now that's a loaded question.

"In a nutshell? I'm hostess for a reality-television program and have to interview my own best friend because she's a contestant on the show. I got my dog wormed, my windows washed and three new tutoring opportunities. My other best friend, Pete, has been cooking dinner for me every night. He says it's because he wants to take care of me, but the real reason is that the woman he's crazy about won't give him the time of day and he can't stay home alone with his thoughts. My parents have announced their plans to stay in an ice hotel in Swedish Lapland this winter. I cleaned my closet and gave most of my clothes to charity. There, how's that?" I didn't mention that I'd also fallen in love with her unavailable neighbor.

"And I chaperoned a group of children to the zoo. Boy, do I feel like an underachiever. Tell me about the television show and your friend," Linda encouraged.

"I can't tell you much. The producers think that in order for our interview to be 'real,' we shouldn't discuss the show before the interview."

"So you don't know if she's going to have a nose job or a body lift? That must be difficult."

I helped myself to a scone and some strawberry jam. "The odd thing is that lately Maggie appears relatively unconcerned about the show. Her mind is elsewhere. Not many weeks ago this was all she wanted out of life and now she seems disinterested in the process."

"Maybe she's decided she's okay with her looks as they are."

"I can't imagine how it could happen. I doubt she'll ever be satisfied."

"Why are *you* doing it, Quinn? You said yourself you wouldn't have taken the job if it weren't for your friend."

"I had this crazy idea I could 'protect' her."

"Maybe she doesn't need your protection."

I silently vowed to bring up the subject of Maggie's changing mood after dinner tonight.

"Have you seen Jack lately?" Linda asked, changing the subject into even more uncomfortable territory.

"Not recently." I felt empty inside as I said it. If Jack *had* been interested in me personally, if he had cared at all, he would have called.

"I'm having him over for dinner this weekend. Want to come?" Linda looked sly and self-satisfied.

"Oh, no you don't. You can't play matchmaker with me. Jack's not interested. I don't want you to put him in an awkward spot."

Unfortunately, Linda didn't have any such reservations.

Chapter Twenty-Six

Seeing Jack so many days after our intimate dinner date gone wrong was as uncomfortable as putting my size-nine feet in size-six shoes. He was charming as always, of course, ready to pull out my chair, ask after my health and smile at my feeble jokes. But there was a vaporous yet impenetrable wall between us that only I seemed to sense, a wall made of memories, of the joy and the grief Jack had experienced with Emily, of all the things I would never ask Jack to put down in order be with me.

When he's ready, I'd been telling myself. I knew I shouldn't fool myself with even that, any longer.

Linda had invited Pete and Maggie to dinner, as well. "The more the merrier," she'd said, and I was grateful for their presence.

"Ben's going to camp next summer," Jack announced over dessert. "He'll be in the pilot for the JA program. It's going to be outstanding."

He turned to me. "He's been in a growth spurt, Quinn. He ate me out of house and home for three weeks and now he's taking off like a weed. Eat, grow, eat, grow. That's how it works with Ben."

"I miss him. I'm glad he's in school and doing well, but I do miss him." How much more stilted could this conversation get?

"He misses you, too. You should stop by and say hello sometime."

And run into you again? That's like taking a bandage off one hair at a time. No thanks.

"I'll call him."

"He'd like that." Something flickered in Jack's eyes. Disappointment? Hardly. Relief.

Then unexpectedly, he added under his breath, "I missed you, too."

Unfortunately, Jack left the party first without offering to walk me to my car.

As I was leaving, Linda backed me into a small powder room just off their foyer and demanded, "What happened? Where'd the magnetic pull between you two go? You're acting like strangers."

A rap on the front door forced Linda and I to spill out of the powder room.

The front door opened. "Linda, I forgot my jacket in the dining room." Jack looked as if there was something he wanted to say but before he could, Maggie breezed in from the other room.

"Oh, good, you haven't left yet," she said to Jack. "You mentioned that you'd never been on a studio set. Why don't you come tomorrow? Quinn is interviewing me."

"Thanks, Maggie, but I have appointments all day tomorrow. I'm sorry."

He glanced at me and looked away. "Really sorry."

"Another time, then."

But of course Jack and I both knew another time wouldn't come.

"Hey, Quinn, how's it going?" Sam greeted me at the studio with his ever present smile. "Are you ready to interview Maggie about her upcoming transformation?"

Sam is the most engaging and likable guy on the studio set. He is also very handsome in his own broken and patched-back-together way. I can see why Maggie enjoyed their time together during the show.

"Not bad, considering. Sam, may I ask you something?"

"Of course. I'm an open book."

"You are, aren't you? What you see is what you get."

He grinned his toothy smile. "I hope it's more than that. What you see isn't that great." He held up a mug. "Coffee? You're early and we're late. We've got time."

I took a mug and sat down out of everyone's way in a darkened corner of the room by a large curtain. "How do you do it? Everybody loves you. Every woman on the set would like to take you home and cook you dinner."

"Is that an invitation?" He leaned back in his own chair and crossed his legs at his ankles. "I don't 'do' anything, Quinn. I'm just me. Simple, steady, ugly me."

"You aren't ugly!"

"Have you looked at me lately? My nose looks toward my left ear, my jaw shoots the other way, I've got a mouth full of ivories that just won't quit and I had terrible acne as a kid. Ugly is my middle name!"

There wasn't anything to say. He hadn't exaggerated, yet when I look at him I see warm eyes, a smile that's spread throughout his entire body, curly black hair, broad shoulders, a trim body and the one of the most beautiful personalities I've ever met.

He saw my confusion. "'Handsome is as handsome does, Sam,' my grandmother used to say. She told me that if the most beautiful person in the world was a bad-tempered liar, their handsomeness would only fool people for a little while. Then others would see them for what they are and they wouldn't be so pretty, anymore."

He took a swig of the coffee. "That bit of knowledge came in handy when I started boxing and got beat up like this. I always figured if I was handsome on the inside, it would show through, like Grandma said."

"And it does."

He smiled endearingly at me. "So I never bothered to get my nose fixed and I'm doing okay." A shadow passed over his features. "That's why it is so hard to work on this particular show.

"These women don't get it. There's not an 'ugly' one in the bunch. Look at Maggie. She's gorgeous. I have no idea what she's doing here." He looked at me shyly. "I'd love to have a woman like Maggie by my side. I'd walk ten feet tall.

"You're a Christian, aren't you?" Sam asked abruptly. "I can tell from things you say and how you act around here. You're just—nice."

"That's a lovely compliment, thank you."

"See, I'm a Christian, too. My grandmother saw to that. She told me that God made me perfect for the purpose He had for me. I didn't believe her for a long time, but lately I've realized she's right."

I leaned forward and felt my elbow bump into something on the other side of the curtain. When I moved again, whatever had been there was gone.

"See, here I am, happy as a clam, with a bunch of discontented women. If they looked like me, *then* they'd have something to be dissatisfied about! Maybe God's trying to make a point here. You know Mandy, the blond lady you interviewed first? She is changing her mind about what she wants to have done."

Sam's eyes sparkled. "She said that talking to you and meeting me proved to her that looks aren't everything. Cool, huh? I just had to wait until God put me and my ugly mug in a place where it could do some good."

I didn't attempt to stop Sam from calling himself ugly because he wore it as a badge of valor rather than of shame.

"I wish Maggie could hear you."

"Hearing isn't enough. She's got to believe I'm telling the truth."

Maggie. After Sam left, I peeked around the curtain to see if I'd knocked something over with my elbow and found Maggie, huddled in a corner, half-hidden by the big sheets of canvas. Tears streaked her face.

For the very first time I thought that *Chrysalis* could do Maggie a little good. She needed someone to powder her nose.

I knelt beside her, put my hands on her shoulders and felt her tremble.

Impulsively, I opened my cell phone and called Pete. "Can you come to the studio and pick Maggie up?"

"Didn't she drive herself? I thought you were taping today."

"Something has come up. Pull up at the side door. I'll have her out there in five minutes."

"Is she okay?"

"She will be if you get over here." I snapped my phone shut and turned back to Maggie.

"I'm taking you out of here."

"The interview…"

"Is off. Come on." I pulled her to her feet and steered her toward the nearest door and made sure no one else saw us.

After I'd stuffed her, weeping again, into Pete's car and given him instructions to take her home and stay with her until I got there, I went back into the studio. Sam and Eddie were looking worried. Frank flapped his arms like a big black raven when he realized Maggie was missing.

"The taping is off. We'll have to try again tomorrow. Maggie isn't up to it. I just sent her home."

"*You* sent her home," Frank blustered. "Who gave you authority to do that?"

"She's not well, Frank. She couldn't string two sentences together. You don't want that on camera, do you?"

He gave a helpless little flutter with his hands. "What about tomorrow?"

"We have other things we can do if she's not able," Sam said.

Frank started to protest but closed his mouth again.

Sam was the go-to guy in this operation. If Sam could work it out, things would be okay. "You'd better go look after Maggie."

By the time I got home, Maggie was in the shower and Pete was striding back and forth across the floor. Dash weaved in and out around him as Pete paced, tripping him up with every other step.

"What went on over there? I'm going to call Eddie and—"

"No need. Eddie and Frank didn't have anything to do with this."

"What then?"

"Your guess is as good as mine. I found her curled up in a ball, sobbing like a baby, so I called you and got her out of there. I told them she wasn't up to the interview and walked out."

"She shouldn't be doing this," Pete muttered. "She's probably come to that conclusion herself. She told me that the plastic surgeons she consulted with won't have anything to do with her."

"Good. It restores my faith in medicine. But that shouldn't make her fall apart like this."

"What would?"

We heard a small scuffling at the door and turned to see Maggie wrapped in fuzzy white terry cloth from head to toe. Her eyes looked like burnt patches in her ashen face.

"I'll tell you," she said softly. "I've done something stupid. I've fallen in love."

Of all the things she could have said, that was the last one I expected.

"I don't want to be in love with this man. I shouldn't be. It makes no sense."

Pete and Dash flopped onto the couch. Maggie and I sat down in the chairs across from them.

"So it's not about the show?"

Maggie passed a hand across her eyes. "The show is the single most stupid thing I could do. I just felt so hurt and awful about Randy and losing the health-club job."

"Don't forget the gray hair," Pete said helpfully.

"I had to do the very dumbest thing I could in order to realize that I was being ridiculous. All this time I've allowed the childhood tape of my sisters' voices tell me I wasn't pretty enough or thin enough. They've grown up and gone on with their lives but I keep opening all the old wounds."

"They were jealous kids, Maggie."

"I had no idea how much I had internalized their hurtful words." She looked agonized. "I've been living my life as if everything they said is true and it's not...it's *not.*"

"What do your sisters have to do with being in love?" Leave it to Pete to bring the conversation back into focus. "And what's so bad about being in love?" He made a strangled sound in the back of his throat. "Unless the person you love acts like you are invisible."

Dash, seeing that Pete was unhappy, tried to crawl into his lap.

"Who is it and why didn't you tell us?"

"And does he know about it?"

Maggie buried her nose in the neck of her robe.

"So this mysterious guy doesn't even know you're attracted to him?"

"I hardly know him and he has no idea how I feel about him. It wouldn't work…we aren't anything alike…I never thought I could imagine myself with someone like him…." And she burst into tears. "I'm a shallow, vain, hypocritical snob!"

That sounded like the start of a very long conversation. Silently I stood up and began to make coffee.

We sat staring into the bottoms of the mugs until Maggie spoke again. "I saw Randy yesterday. I met his new girlfriend."

Pete groaned and covered his face.

"She's very nice. Not what I'd expected, though."

I recalled Pete's description of her.

"She even suggested that Randy and I take a few minutes alone to talk." Maggie scrubbed at her hair with the towel before pulling it away, letting her dark locks fall in a fan across the white shoulders of her robe. "He apologized for hurting me."

"As well he should."

"Then I asked him why he broke up with me." Her eyes started to shine with tears again. "He said he didn't think we'd work as a couple because my looks got in the way."

I saw red. "That's why you thought you weren't pretty enough? Because Randy didn't like your looks? The man has to be blind."

"Oh, he loves how I look. What he didn't love was how much time I spent obsessing about myself. He said he was uncomfortable about the way I put myself down and was so focused on my appearance that it ruined our time together. His new girlfriend makes him laugh and she doesn't care if her hair is messy or her nose is sunburned when they go out on his boat," Maggie marveled. "She accepts herself the way she is and he does, too.

"I spent so much time trying to look like I thought he wanted me to look that I ruined the relationship we had. He was right. I was a narcissistic nincompoop. Now my confidence is shot and I can't face the most wonderful man in the world!"

"You did face Randy," Pete pointed out. "Kristy will barely speak to me."

"It's not Randy I'm worried about, anymore," she said obliquely.

Maggie took a tissue from the box on the table nearby and blew her nose, eyes watering and looking miserable. But before she could speak, the doorbell rang.

When I opened it, I was in for another surprise. Jack Harmon stood on the other side of the door.

Chapter Twenty-Seven

"My head hurts," I announced to no one in particular as I waved Jack into the room.

"Don't mind us." I poured him a cup of coffee. "We're in the midst of trying to figure out what's happening in Maggie's love life and so far it's not going well."

To his credit, Jack nodded, took the coffee and sat down at the table, out of Maggie's line of sight. A man who can listen. Dash immediately went to check him out and, to my surprise, settled across Jack's feet and went to sleep. From Dash, that's unqualified approval.

"Now that you've taken this conversation to a whole new dimension, no, an entirely new universe, you'd better explain," Pete demanded.

Follow along and you'll catch up, I mouthed to Jack.

Maggie curled up on the edge of the couch, looking fragile and miserable.

"I thought I was smarter than this."

"You're plenty smart, Mags."

"Yeah? Then why didn't I get it when you two kept talking about being beautiful 'from the inside out'? Why did I think that my whole life would improve if I were different?

"It wasn't until I met the other contestants on *Chrysalis* and heard them running themselves down that it occurred to me that I had things turned around. Those women are fabulous. They are kind, funny, caring and compassionate. I've made great friends. In my eyes they couldn't be prettier.

"Quinn said it all along but I refused to listen. If you're not good with yourself on the inside, you will never be truly beautiful. Instead, you'll be like an empty snail shell with its lovely curves and alluring colors but no life inside."

She turned to look at Jack. "And your little boy taught me a thing or two. When he showed me his room the day we were at your house, he started telling me how it was to have arthritis. He showed me his hands. The knuckles were red and swollen and he told me they were sore that day. Then he said something that opened my eyes. He told me he was lucky because he didn't hurt everyday, because he'd had a 'really great mom' until he was eight and because his dad loved him so much.

"I felt so shallow that I could hardly face myself after I met Ben. I lost a boyfriend and a job, not my health! Ben made me realize how egotistic and self-absorbed I've been."

"Ben has opened my eyes a time or two, as well," Jack assured her.

"But that's not the worst of it," she went on. "I'd quit

praying because I'd decided even God wouldn't want anything to do with me. I gave up the one thing I've had to rely on my entire life, the assurance that He'd get me through."

She threw her head backward against the couch and groaned. "Well, He got me good for that one."

The three of us leaned forward in our chairs. "What do you mean 'got you'?"

"Me, the woman who thought no one would love me if I wasn't perfect? The person who thought beauty was everything? When I finally got down on my knees and did ask God to help me, what did He do?"

"What?" we said in unison.

"He gave me Sam Waters."

"What's so bad about that?"

I've been so blind that I'm furious with myself.

"I've fallen in love with him!"

Jack stood up and moved into our circle and sat down beside me. "What's so special about this Sam guy?"

Pete burst out laughing. "Nothing! Nothing is special about Sam! He is ordinary, kind, generous, gentle, plain-spoken and salt of the earth. He says himself he's got a face like a mud fence, he loves to work behind the scenes instead of in the limelight and he's perfectly content with his life."

Now Jack looked thoroughly confused.

"Don't you see? Maggie didn't think anyone could fall in love with her if she didn't have makeup on. And here she is, crazy about a guy who wouldn't change a thing about himself, broken nose and all. She's in love with the man he is, not his outside shell. It's a God 'gotcha'!"

Pete looked at Maggie with affection. "It's the lesson that you had to learn for yourself, isn't it, Mags? That if a person's heart is good, how he looks doesn't matter."

She grabbed another tissue and blew her nose so hard she honked.

Maggie brought an entire entourage with her to the taping of our interview—Pete, Jack, Ben and Dash. Sam just grinned and shook his head as he saw the crowd gathering around us.

"Sit over there," he instructed. "And keep the dog quiet."

"Maggie's a little freaked today and Dash is her doggy tranquilizer," I explained.

"He's good then. I'm a believer in natural medicine." Sam glanced in Maggie's direction. "Will she be okay?"

"She told me she's looking forward to telling the *Chrysalis* audience about her experience."

She just isn't so fine with having fallen in love with you, Sam. That's rocked her world.

Dash began to squirm and whine at my feet. "I think he has to go out, Pete."

Pete looked at the dog askance. "If I take him out now they won't let me in while they are taping. I want to see you and Maggie."

Dash did the doggy shuffle and butted his head against Pete's leg, a blatant request for a walk.

"Can't you just wait, buddy? Half an hour? I'll give you a treat if—"

"You're talking to a dog, Peter." A soft, slightly disgruntled voice interrupted him. "You may think you can bargain with people, but dogs don't negotiate."

Kristy Bessett walked up to Dash and stroked his head. Dash lost all interest in Pete and glommed onto Kristy as his new best opportunity for a walk.

"I'll take you, big boy," Kristy said soothingly. "I can see a taping anytime." She picked up the leash attached to Dash's collar and walked him calmly toward the door.

"Wait!" Pete yelped, but Kristy kept moving. As she went through the door that led to the parking lot, he went after her. A stagehand, shaking his head, locked the door behind them.

The *Chrysalis* set reminds me of a stop on the migration pattern of monarch butterflies from Canada to Mexico. They'd gone all out with the butterfly theme. Even the chairs where Maggie and I would sit for the interview had a split back shaped into two soft arches like butterfly wings. Somehow it looked more elegant that kitschy. That was no doubt thanks to Sam's keen eye.

As they did a final touch-up on our makeup, Maggie and I stared at each other. Finally I would hear what had been going on in Maggie's life and head these past days.

"Everybody quiet on the set. Ten, nine, eight…"

As the lights around us dimmed, we were suffused in a pool of bright light, an island in the darkened room.

Of all the women I'd interviewed on the show so far, Maggie was the easiest—and the most difficult. The others were benefiting from the makeover they were receiving, but although she wasn't wearing any makeup, there was no way to hide her innate beauty. With her hair pulled back from her face and in a dark turtleneck sweater, she looked more like a cross between Sophia Loren and Audrey Hepburn than a candidate for a makeover.

Much to my surprise, she said as much.

"Why, Maggie, did you decide that you would be a good contestant for *Chrysalis?* It's apparent to our audience that you are a beautiful woman. Many of them are no doubt wondering what you are doing here." I could imagine Frank snarling as I asked the question.

Maggie leaned forward and looked past me at the camera hovering near my shoulder that was filming her face. "I decided for all the wrong reasons."

"The wrong reasons?" I echoed, surprised.

"I'd just broken up with my boyfriend and I was feeling really low. Even though I'm a model, I thought he wasn't interested in me any longer because of my looks. I'd convinced myself that in order to be loved I had to be beautiful. Therefore, if he didn't love me anymore, I must no longer be beautiful. Then I lost two modeling jobs that were very important to me. That only confirmed that something was going terribly wrong.

"I've hung my self-esteem on how I look my entire life." Her face was intent, her eyes focused and I knew that she was talking not to me but to the audience who would tune in to see the show. "Even though I grew up hearing 'God loves you' and 'You're perfect in His sight,' I didn't buy it. I dieted until I passed out. I exercised for hours every day. I pored over books about hair, clothes and makeup. I decided the way to prove to myself that I was pretty was to be a model. Every decision I've ever made had something to do with making me feel better in here." She thumped on her chest with her fist. "And I thought the way to do that was—" she ran a graceful finger along the side of her face "—was to change something out here."

"How does *Chrysalis* play into all of this?"

I was completely extraneous to whatever message Maggie was trying to get across. Standing at the edge of the circle of light, I could see Frank frowning and chewing on his fingernails. This was not what he'd wanted to happen.

"I was still in the I-can-fix-this-from-the-outside mode when I auditioned. I'm not sure why I was chosen, but I'm glad I was."

"What have the rounds of interviews with stylists, surgeons and trainers taught you?"

"That I'm just fine the way I am."

A buzz broke out in the back of the room and I saw Eddie restraining Frank, who wanted to stop taping.

"That doesn't mean this show hasn't been special to me," she hurried to add, "because it has. I did come out of my chrysalis. I was hidden in an ugly cocoon of low self-esteem. I'm emotionally and spiritually new and without this program I don't know if I ever would have been.

"This show taught me that I needed to get over myself and to see the shallowness of physical beauty without a soul to match. Because of this show and the prayers of my friends and God's grace, now I have beauty in my spirit. *That's* what I want people to know now."

Tears ran down my cheeks and the cameraman moved in for a close-up.

Maggie, still not out of surprises, stared past me into the darkness where Sam stood. "I'll never judge someone by their appearance again. I lived in an emotional wasteland. I actually believed I was humble because I thought so little of myself. I realize now that that is the most egocentric, vain attitude of all."

"Maggie," I said impulsively. "Is there anything you'd like to say to the producers of *Chrysalis?*"

"Just thank you. I didn't change on the outside like you expected, but there's a whole new person in here." She put her hand over her heart and the lights came up in the room. It was so silent that the room felt as though it were holding its breath. Then the crew erupted in cheers.

I listened to snippets of conversation as they ping-ponged around the room. The reaction was positive all around. *He did it,* I thought. *He did it! God came to reality television!*

I turned to talk to Maggie but she was gone. It was Jack walking toward me with a huge grin on his face.

"Looks like you may have invented a new genre here," he commented. "Internal makeover shows."

"Not me, Maggie. She blew me away. I had no idea what she was planning."

"I could tell. You were beaming at her like a floodlight. Your producers are ecstatic. The one who looks like Count Chocula was actually smiling. This will be a good shocker for the show."

"I want to tell Maggie how amazing she was."

"Frankly, I don't think she's interested in hearing it right now." Jack pointed to a far corner of the studio. Maggie and Sam were wrapped in each other's arms. "He came and scooped her up as soon as they quit filming. She started crying and telling him he was the best-looking guy in the world. Next thing I know, they're off in the corner whispering."

Jack grinned and took my hand. "Congratulations, Madame Moderator, I think you may have a new hit on your hands."

The congratulatory lovefest went on for some time before I noticed that Pete was missing and Eddie wandered over to ask where his sister had gone. It was then I remembered Dash and the fact that a stagehand had locked them outside before the taping.

Eddie and I raced to the door and flung it open.

"Hey, sorry. I didn't know you guys got locked out. You could have gone to the reception area." Then Eddie looked more closely at his sister. "You've got a goofy look on your face, Kris." He turned to stare at Pete. "But it's no goofier than yours. What's been going on out here?"

Dash woofed and dodged inside as if he'd had enough kissing and making up to last a doggy lifetime.

"Oh, brother," Eddie groaned. "Don't tell me!"

"That's right," Pete said, not breaking his gaze with Kristy. "I'm going to be your brother. Well, brother-in-law technically, but same thing, don't you think?" He bent to kiss Kristy.

"It's about time," Eddie grumbled to me. "I thought Kristy was going to ignore him forever even though it was killing her. She was scared of letting him know she still had feelings for him, because she figured he'd have dozens of women after him now."

I looked at the besotted pair in the entry. "I don't think Kristy has a thing to worry about."

* * *

"I'm glad I came to the studio." Jack commented as we said good-night. "I didn't expect so much to happen."

"Nor did I." I couldn't help grinning.

Pete and Kristy had gone off immediately to look at wedding rings. Never let it be said that Pete doesn't learn from his mistakes. He's not going to let her get away this time.

Sam and Maggie were still at the studio when we left, holding hands and gazing raptly into each other's eyes.

"It wouldn't surprise me if we had two weddings in the very near future."

Chapter Twenty-Eight

"It's another Saturday with just you and me, Dash. What do you feel like doing? Going out for a burger at the drive-through? Watching a movie? Working out?"

I looked at him as he gazed up at me, his tail wagging back and forth like a metronome. "How pathetic is this? I'm asking a dog what he wants to do on a Saturday afternoon."

His wagging increased, obviously to indicate his full agreement with my seriously pitiful state.

Pete and Kristy are absolutely no company whatsoever, lost as they are in their own little world. Maggie and Sam aren't much better. Sam is as deeply in love with Maggie as she is with him. They are already starting to read each other's minds and finish each other's sentences.

I'm delighted, of course, but it has left an enormous hole in my social life. I've quit hoping that Jack will call since he performed another vanishing act and I haven't seen him all week.

I've never been so piteously grateful to hear the phone ring as I was today.

Ben was on the other end of the line, burbling like a running stream. "Nathan's mom let him adopt a greyhound and we're going to look at some, too!"

Jack took the phone from his son. "Tell me I need to have my head examined."

"Your head is fine. I think it's wonderful that you're going to adopt a dog."

"What makes you think we'll adopt one? I just told Ben that he could *look* at them."

"When you go looking for a pet you'll always find one," I warned. "Don't take him looking if you don't plan to bring one home."

"Would you and Dash like to come with us?" Jack surprised me with the question. He's been as distant as Istanbul lately, so this was not what I'd expected.

"Sure. But Dash? Are you sure that's wise?"

"Ben wants him to sit in the backseat with him."

"Dash is always ready for a car ride, but you don't have to—"

"We want to. Pick you up in thirty minutes."

Thirty minutes. I changed clothes three times, paced the length of my house, chewed off a fingernail and still had plenty of time to wonder why Jack had called now. I also had time to get angry.

"I'm tired of being convenient," I said to Dash as he sat patiently by the door in his red doggy sweater. "He only calls when Ben wants to do something with me and it's never going to change. What's the point? He's married to a memory and I'm the last person in the world willing to try to break that up."

I paced some more and Dash whined and lay down on the rug. "What's wrong with me? Why don't I feel like going out and doing things? I don't believe in sitting around and waiting for a telephone to ring. I should have just told him no, Dash. *N-O,* no."

And why haven't I? Because I love him and I'm not the least bit happy about it. Jack's not going to change. He's going to be charming, funny, pleasant to be with and single for the rest of his life.

If I had a brain in my head, I'd accept that as fact and move on.

"I'm going to tell him, Dash. I won't be available anymore for impulse outings at his convenience. We need to put a stop to this. I don't want to be his buddy. I want to be his…" The thought hit me like a hammer. "I want to be his wife."

But first we had to look at a greyhound.

"Nathan's mom says there are three to pick from," Ben greeted me as I let Dash into the backseat with him. They're all ready for good homes. We'd be a good home, Dad."

"Don't get your hopes up, son. I said we'd look, nothing more."

Ben looked at me and winked. I winked back. We'd allow Jack to live in his fantasyland just a little bit longer.

We walked into the dog's current foster home and were left speechless. Three incredibly sleek, elegant dogs were standing there looking as us with what, I swear, was hope in their eyes.

"The black one is Midnight. We call him Middy. The little girl in the middle, the brindle, is Princess and the male on the end is Daffy, which pretty much explains his personality." The woman who had greeted us leaned over to scratch Daffy's ears. "I've had a call from a family who is interested in adopting two dogs, so if you are interested in one of these, you can have your pick.

"I'm fussy about who the dogs go to, so we'd do a background check, just to make sure it gets a good home, but the dogs are ready to start their new lives." She rubbed the underside of Daffy's chin. "Aren't you, big guy?"

"We have a greyhound in the car," Ben said. "Would you like to see him? His name is Dash." And before we could stop him, Ben went out the door and down the sidewalk to the van.

"We don't have to bring him in," I began.

"I don't mind. Then you'll see if your dog is well matched with one of these. You want them to be compatible."

Our dog? This woman thought we were a family.

Ben returned with Dash.

"I'll leave you alone," the woman said. "I'll be in the kitchen if you need me. Take your time. When I foster dogs, I fall in love with them. I don't want you to take a dog that you haven't fallen for, too."

Within minutes, Dash had made his selection.

"He likes Midnight," Ben gasped. "Look at them."

Dash and Midnight had lain down together on the rug and tangled themselves together much as Dash and Flash do.

"That's lovely," I pointed out to Ben, "but you have to pick the dog *you* like best, not Dash."

To my surprise, Ben looked at his father and said in a very adult voice, "Dad…"

Jack cleared his throat and shuffled his feet uncomfortably.

"You promised," Ben chided as if he were the father and Jack his son. "It's *okay.*"

"I think that Dash should like the dog Ben picks out," Jack said with a catch in his voice. "Ben and I have been talking about a lot of things lately." His eyes flashed with something I couldn't decipher. "We've talked about his mother and how we miss her. We've talked about our life and how empty it's been without her. And we talked about how it is to be in love with two people and yet be true to both of them."

Something in his tone held me firmly frozen to the spot.

"Ben and I have been a team for over two years now and we've made all our decisions about our family together. Ben and I decided that if you were willing to understand how we feel about Ben's mom and not mind sharing her memory with us, that maybe…just maybe… Dash and Ben's new dog could live under the same roof. And if that were the case, it would be very important to have Dash's opinion today, don't you think?"

"Was that…is that…a *proposal?*" I blurted.

Ben sighed, rolled his eyes and came to stand in front of his father. "He didn't do it like we practiced," the little boy told me. "He's been worried that I wouldn't want another mom 'cause I had such a good one in the first place. But I told him that getting another good mom was fine with me. I'll always love my first mom, no matter what."

Ben shot his father a reproving look. "Here's how we practiced it." Ben took my hand and said, "Quinn, will you marry m—" He paused. Then he put my hand into Jack's. "Quinn, will you marry my dad?"

And as Jack and I stood there speechless, Ben, the little professor and expert at love said, "That's how it goes, Dad. Now, you try it."

"Quinn," Jack began.

I put my finger to his lips. "Yes, I will."

And before either of us could move, Ben whooped and began to tug on my shirt. When I bent toward him, he kissed me on the cheek with a loud smacking sound.

"And that's how you do *that,* Dad.'

As if waking from a trance, Jack pulled me close. "Thanks for the input, Ben, but I can take it from here."

And he did.

* * * * *

Look for SLEEPING BEAUTY by Judy Baer,
available in October from Love Inspired.

And turn the page for a sneak preview of
Judy's THE BABY CHRONICLES, the sequel to
The Whitney Chronicles available September 2007
from Steeple Hill Books.

March 1

My assistant, Mitzi, canceled the office waiting room subscriptions to *Vogue* and *Elle* and replaced them with *Fit Pregnancy* and *American Baby*. I realize now that I should have appreciated it when she was only giving me fashion advice.

Frankly, the one magazine Mitzi should be allowed to read is her signature publication, *Harper's Bazarre*.

My name is Whitney Blake Andrews, and today I'm starting a new volume of my personal journal. It's been quite a ride since that first day two years ago when I began keeping what I fondly call *The Whitney Chronicles*. My best friend, Kim Easton, has overcome breast cancer and her son Wesley has turned three. I've been made vice-president of Innova Software and have been married for almost two years to Dr. Chase Andrews, the most incredible husband in the universe. That's my personal bias, of course.

And Mitzi Fraisier is still the most aggravating person on this planet, but she's *my* aggravating person, so I love her, anyway. Most of the time…at least, some of the time…in brief spurts… Hmm…I *do* remember having a pleasant thought about her sometime between last Christmas and New Year's Eve. I think.

Kim stopped over after work tonight so that we could debrief our day at the office. She likes to come to my house for three reasons. There are no Legos imbedded in the carpet, Ernie and Elmo are not the anchormen during the evening news and there is always chocolate.

I've been sacrificing myself in the name of medical science, researching the curative uses for chocolate. It has the same health promoting chemicals as fruits and veggies. It's the least I can do for the good of mankind. How often did I dream Mom would tell me to eat my chocolate cake instead of my brussels sprouts?

"Men are wired differently from women," Kim said. "I see it in Wesley already. He and his dad spend hours piling blocks into pyramids and knocking them down. They laugh and high-five each other like they've just invented football. Yet when I ask Kurt to vacuum the floor he says, 'Didn't I just do that *last* month?' as if he detests repetition in any form."

"Knocking things down and picking things up are two entirely different concepts. One is male, the other, female. Even Chase says so."

Chase. Two years of marriage and I love him more than ever. God really knew what He was doing when He put us together. It doesn't hurt that his sandy hair is shot with gold, his eyes an inky, Crayola blue and his physique—there's only one way to describe it—hunky. Oh, yes, and he's crazy about me and he's a doctor. This morning he sent me yellow roses for no reason at all except that he loves me.

"Now you're thinking about *him*," Kim observed grumpily. "You've got that moonstruck look on your face again."

"And you don't feel that way about Kurt anymore?" I teased.

"Of course I do." Kim's attention drifted from me into some private thought of her own. "I wish…"

"Wish what?" I held the candy dish under her nose to refocus her with the scent of chocolate.

"Kurt and I have been talking lately about—" Kim reached in and took a piece of Dove dark chocolate, fortifying herself for a heavy-duty conversation "—having another baby."

My stomach took a roller-coaster ride from peak to valley and up again.

"Wesley will love a baby brother or sister! That's wonderful…"

Frankly, Wesley has become a bit of a tyrant, having control of two entire households as he does—Kim's and mine. It wouldn't hurt a bit to have a new baby around, someone who instinctively knows how to establish a dictatorship. It may seem absurd to think of a baby as a despot, but I can't think of an autocrat more qualified to put Wes in his place.

My excitement evaporated when I saw the expression on Kim's face. "Isn't it?"

"Of course it is!" she blurted, and burst into tears.

At that moment, a flurry of activity erupted as my cats, Mr. Tibble and Scram, growling and hissing, rolled together past our feet like an absurd kitty volleyball.

"Ignore them," I advised.

"Won't they hurt themselves doing that?" Kim snuffled.

As she spoke, Mr. Tibble tired of the game and went limp, as if his bones had liquefied. Scram tumbled halfway across the room by himself before he realized he'd been abandoned, stood up and marched off huffily, his tail straight in the air in a gesture of disdain.

I'd insulted Mr. Tibble deeply when I introduced Scram into his peaceful kingdom, but he took on the kitten with aplomb, taught him who was boss and generally made Scram a subservient being to his own royalty. Just like what Mitzi tries to do with us at work.

"So tell me about this new-baby conversation," I urged, "and why it makes you cry."

"If we don't hurry up, Wesley will be grown up. I don't want a large age gap between him and a baby brother or sister."

There's not much danger of being all grown up when one still sucks his thumb, refuses to sleep without his blankie and demands Cheerios in church, but when Kim is emotional, logic flies out the window.

"What's stopping you?"

Kim looked pained. "Kurt is worried about my health. He's been on the Internet trying to find out if getting pregnant with my personal history of breast cancer will increase the risk of the cancer recurring."

"And?"

"If the cancer returns while I'm pregnant, treatment options are limited. Chemotherapy can be given without hurting the baby, but it's not given in the first trimester, when the major organs are forming. Kurt knows I'd never do anything to harm the baby, even if it were risky for me. He's afraid of my having a recurrence. He doesn't want me putting my own life on the line." She rolled her eyes helplessly. "He's been spouting information about hormones like they were football statistics."

"Is the danger real?"

"It is definitely real in Kurt's mind."

"Accept the authority of your husband," I murmured. "There's the rub."

"That might be a thorny issue for some, but to me that means voluntary compromise and teamwork with someone I love and respect. Kurt and I have discussed it. Whatever we decide is a mutual decision." She looked troubled. "But he has even stronger feelings than I. He's convinced I would be inviting problems if I had another baby right now. He's also afraid that being pregnant might exacerbate my depression."

Not a minor concern considering Kim's history.

"He wants to have another child, but not at the expense of my health. He's adamant about that." Tears welled in her eyes. "The idea of not giving birth again breaks my heart! I desperately want to have a brother or sister for Wesley."

"Aren't you putting the cart before the horse? Who

says you won't? Besides, is this about giving birth or about being a parent? There are other ways to…"

But she didn't seem to hear me.

After she left, I put lasagna into the oven, tore up lettuce for salad and still had over an hour before Chase was due to arrive home from work. I couldn't get Kim out of my mind. How would it be to be caught in the place in which Kim found herself? Another child or her health. What would it serve if having another child deprived Wesley of his mother?

To distract myself I picked up our wedding photo album. Looking at those pictures always turns me into a slobbering romantic. When Chase arrived for dinner, I met him at the door holding his slippers and a newspaper and doing my most seductive siren imitation. Unfortunately his cousin's dog, Winslow, had made hash of his slippers last weekend, and to find them I'd had to dig through the garbage can. Fortunately, they didn't smell *too* bad Since we both read the paper at work, I'd also had to substitute an *O* magazine for the *Tribune.*

Clever man. He knew immediately that something was up.

"Now what have you and Kim been doing?" he asked as he put his arms around my waist and gathered me to him. "Last time you tried the newspaper and slippers routine on me, you'd agreed to foster a potential seeing-eye puppy without talking to me first."

"Did you even consider that might be because I love you and I want to show it?"

"No." He grinned and his dimples deepened. "I know

you love me. You show it every day and in every way. Something else is going on."

I ran my finger along the chiseled line of his jaw and was supremely thankful to have this man in my life. *Blessed. I am so blessed.*

I stared into the inky blueness of his eyes and watched them grow round with surprise as I whispered, "Chase, how do you feel about having a baby?"

* * * * *

Dear Reader,

As you may be able to tell from *Mirror, Mirror* and many of my other books, I am an animal lover. I chose to give adopted greyhounds to Quinn and Pete, and all my research on greyhounds shows them to be sweet, docile, loving and wonderful pets. There are so many of these beautiful former racing dogs available for adoption that I used them to encourage others to consider this breed when seeking a new pet. Adopting a pet is both one of the kindest and most satisfying things an individual can do. Providing a home for an animal that might otherwise not be allowed to live, and in return being lavished with love, attention and devotion is highly gratifying.

I've had many pets over the years, owned buffalo and horses and had a surprisingly pleasant and animated relationship with a goldfish rescued from a centerpiece at a wedding reception. Animals bring richness, love and humor to peoples' lives. They deserve respect and affection, like the kind Flash and Dash received from the characters in my book.

I hope you enjoy *Mirror, Mirror* and that it makes you contemplate the qualities of beauty. I'm sure that those you think most beautiful are lovely from the inside out.

Blessings,

Judy

QUESTIONS FOR DISCUSSION

1. How much of your self-esteem and that of others you know is based on how you look? Please explain.

2. If money or safety were no object, would you have plastic surgery? Why or why not?

3. Quinn, Pete and Maggie have a friendship that withstands many kinds of emotional weather. Do you have friends like that? What things have you withstood together?

4. Jack is reluctant to date because he feels unfaithful to his first wife. Do you know someone who has ever felt this way? How can you move on when you've lost someone you love?

5. Dash and Flash are adopted greyhounds. Have you ever considered adopting a greyhound or any other pet? Would you consider adopting a greyhound after reading this book?

6. Why is Maggie so stunned to find herself attracted to a man who is not handsome? What character traits do you think she should look for in a person? How much do looks really count in a relationship?

7. Quinn does not appear to pursue modeling jobs, and yet they come to her. Why do you think that is? Have you ever known anyone who exudes an air of desperation like Maggie? How does it make you want to respond to that person?

8. What do you think of reality television shows? Should there be more or fewer of them? Why?

9. Maggie never feels that she looks good enough. How would you feel if you looked like Maggie? Would good looks actually be the answer to your problems?

10. What do you think of Jack's son, Ben? What makes him such a wise little boy? Tell of times when children you know seemed to have more wisdom than the adults around them.

Love Inspired®

REQUEST YOUR FREE BOOKS!

2 FREE INSPIRATIONAL NOVELS
PLUS 2
FREE
MYSTERY GIFTS

LoveInspired

YES! Please send me 2 FREE Love Inspired® novels and my 2 FREE mystery gifts. After receiving them, if I don't wish to receive any more books, I can return the shipping statement marked "cancel." If I don't cancel, I will receive 4 brand-new novels every month and be billed just $3.99 per book in the U.S., or $4.74 per book in Canada, plus 25¢ shipping and handling per book and applicable taxes, if any*. That's a savings of 20% off the cover price! I understand that accepting the 2 free books and gifts places me under no obligation to buy anything. I can always return a shipment and cancel at any time. Even if I never buy another book from Steeple Hill, the two free books and gifts are mine to keep forever.

113 IDN EF26 313 IDN EF27

Name	(PLEASE PRINT)	
Address		Apt. #
City	State/Prov.	Zip/Postal Code

Signature (if under 18, a parent or guardian must sign)

Order online at www.LoveInspiredBooks.com

Or mail to Steeple Hill Reader Service™:

IN U.S.A.: P.O. Box 1867, Buffalo, NY 14240-1867
IN CANADA: P.O. Box 609, Fort Erie, Ontario L2A 5X3

Not valid to current Love Inspired subscribers.

**Want to try two free books from another series?
Call 1-800-873-8635 or visit www.morefreebooks.com**

* Terms and prices subject to change without notice. NY residents add applicable sales tax. Canadian residents will be charged applicable provincial taxes and GST. This offer is limited to one order per household. All orders subject to approval. Credit or debit balances in a customer's account(s) may be offset by any other outstanding balance owed by or to the customer. Please allow 4 to 6 weeks for delivery.

Your Privacy: Steeple Hill is committed to protecting your privacy. Our Privacy Policy is available online at www.eHarlequin.com or upon request from the Reader Service. From time to time we make our lists of customers available to reputable firms who may have a product or service of interest to you. If you would prefer we not share your name and address, please check here. ☐

LIREG07

Love Inspired®

Celebrate Love Inspired's 10th anniversary with top authors and great stories all year long!

FROM BESTSELLING AUTHOR
JILLIAN HART
COMES A NEW McKASLIN CLAN STORY.

THE McKASLIN CLAN

Lauren McKaslin wanted to reconnect with her family, but mistrustful lawman Caleb Stone stood in her way. Was his attention more than a protective instinct? Now that she believed in family again, perhaps this was also the time to believe in true love.

Look for
A McKASLIN HOMECOMING

Love Inspired®
Jillian Hart
A McKaslin Homecoming

THE McKASLIN CLAN

Available July wherever you buy books.

Steeple Hill®

www.SteepleHill.com

LIAMHJH

TITLES AVAILABLE NEXT MONTH

Don't miss these four stories in July

A McKASLIN HOMECOMING by Jillian Hart
The McKaslin Clan

Lauren McKaslin wanted to reconnect with her family, but mistrustful lawman Caleb Stone stood in her way. Was his attention more than a protective instinct? Now that she believed in family again, perhaps this was also the time to believe in true love.

FOR HER SON'S LOVE by Kathryn Springer
A Tiny Blessings Tale

With the legality of her son's adoption in question, Miranda Jones knows she can't trust anyone in Chestnut Grove with her secrets—especially Andrew Noble. He was working his way into her heart, but his investigation into her past could tear her family apart.

THE PERFECT BLEND by Allie Pleiter
A special Steeple Hill Café novel in Love Inspired

Opening a coffee shop was Maggie Black's dream. She just had to get a loan. Banker William Grey III wanted her to take his business class first, and Maggie agreed. After all, his velvety British accent could make even financial analysis sound interesting.

THE HEART'S FORGIVENESS by Merrillee Whren
Single father Grady Reynolds moved his family to Pinecrest for a fresh start. Instead he found a reminder of the past in Maria Sanchez. She thought helping Grady regain his lost faith would be easy. Except Grady wasn't ready to give or receive forgiveness…or love.

LICNM0607